The Elmore Leonard Reader

Elmore Leonard

SELECTIONS FROM

STICK
SPLIT IMAGES
CAT CHASER
CITY PRIMEVAL
52 PICK-UP
UNKNOWN MAN #89

AVON BOOKS
A division of
The Hearst Corporation
1790 Broadway
New York, N.Y. 10019

STICK

"The pace is blistering, and nobody but nobody writes better dialogue. One of the season's grabbers. Grab it." <u>New York Daily News</u>

Leonard's newest bestseller is a brisk, tough suspense novel about an ex-con living in Florida's flashy Gold Coast, who is fresh out of prison and right into a high-rolling—and deadly—scam.

Soon to be a major motion picture! Starring and directed by Burt Reynolds. Sold to Universal Pictures for a whopping $350,000, it will also star Candice Bergen and George Segal. Elmore Leonard has written the screenplay for the film which is shooting now on location in Florida. Scheduled for release in late 1984, STICK is being produced by Jennings Lang.

Coming in March

The following excerpt is from Chapter 5...

Rainy, behind the wheel of the Chevy van, would glance at Stick as he spoke and from Stick back to the four lanes of freeway and the red taillights moving in the dark.

"The way I understand it, Chucky owes the money because it was his fault Nestor Soto had to put up a bond, the two-hundred thousand, to get one of his guys out. Then when the guy left and went to Colombia it was okay with Nestor because he say Chucky has to pay him. See, Chucky knew a guy from New York or some place he thought was a good guy. He see him in the Mutiny, different places, he knows the guy is buying product, right? Now this guy tells Chucky he wants to make a big buy—I don't know how many kilos, man— I'm talking about coke. So Chucky is thinking okay, no problem. He'll broker the deal, put the guy in touch with Nestor Soto and make about five-ten percent from the guy, everybody's happy, right? Except what do you know, this guy from New York, man, he turns out he's a deep narc, man, from the BNDD. Sure, he put it together, they raid this place Nestor has down in Homestead on the canal, kill one of his guys, bust the other one—that's the two-hundred-thousand bond—take all his shit, man, and Nestor believe Chucky put the stuff on him. What else is he going to think? Nestor is crazy anyway. Sometime they call him El Chaco, from some wild place where he was born. El Chaco. He believe in *santería,*man, like voodoo. He start free-basing, he kill these animals as a sacrifice, with a knife. It can scare the shit out of you, you see something like that. Chucky explain it to him, no, man, he was surprised as Nestor the guy was a narc. He say, ask anybody at the Mutiny, they tell you. Nestor, he finally say okay, but Chucky has to pay him for the bond, you know, that Nestor lost."

"Forfeitted," Stick said.

"Yeah, forfeit. The court don't give it back. So that's it, man, in the suitcase. He always say that, Chucky? About the gorilla." Rainy grinned. "Oh, man..."

"Why'd he pick you?"

"What, to take it? He ask me."

"He's got all those guys—why didn't he send one of them with it?"

"I tell him I need a job, some money. So..."

Stick thought about it, trying to accept Chucky doing Rainy a favor. "What's he on?"

Rainy glanced over. "Who, Chucky? 'Ludes, man. You can tell, uh? How he moves?"

"Like he's walking in mud," Stick said.

Following 95 through Miami, Stick couldn't believe all the cement that had been poured since he was last here, when he was married and living here...He had begun thinking about his former wife, Mary Lou, when Rainy had to brake hard in traffic not watching his lane, and Stick felt his bucket seat slide forward and had to plant his feet. His wife's Camaro had had a seat like that. He would adjust it, there, but it would break loose within a few days and give them something to discuss when his wife wasn't complaining about the hot weather, about not seeing her friends, about her mother driving her crazy...till they moved back to Detroit and she began complaining about the cold, busing, about the colored taking over the shopping malls. Now she was back here again, Stick believed, because she missed bitching about her mother. They were a great pair, with their mouths turned down and set that way for all time. He hoped it wouldn't hurt his little girl, always hearing the negative side of things. His little girl's name was Katy. She had sent him handmade birthday and Father's Day cards, her school pictures some years, and twenty letters during the time he was in prison; more than half of them written when she was twelve. He'd call tomorrow...get a present for her...

They left the freeway and after that Stick didn't know where they were, somewhere in South Miami; all the streets, up-down and across were numbers. Finally Rainy turned a corner at Southwest Seventy-Third Street and pulled up in front of a place with a sign that said Neon Leon's. They had to meet a guy here, Rainy said, who would tell them where to go. A guy name Moke.

Stick said, "Why don't you give him the bag? Get it over with."

"I have to give it to Nestor Soto or his father-in-law, a guy name Avilanosa, nobody else," Rainy said. "Nestor don't advertise, I have to find out where he is...Lock your door."

Stick watched Rainy go into the place—a lounge or a restaurant, it looked new, whatever it was, flashy. *Neon Leon's*. Hot shit. Places like this and Wolfgang's made Stick tired thinking about them. He was getting old. Getting on and nothing to show for it. He'd earned five dollars a week in Jackson as a clerk-porter in the Guidance Center office, filing, mopping floors, cleaning toilets, and managed to come out with 680 dollars. A hundred and a half to get to Florida; a week paid in advance at the Hotel Bon-Aire on South Beach...he had about three hundred left. He'd go as high as a grand from Rainy for sitting here in the dark guarding Chucky's suitcase with almost a quarter of a million in it. Christ...

Moke came out, let go of the door and Rainy had to catch it. Stick watched him approach his side of the van as Rainy came around and got back in.

"He's going with us."

When Stick opened the door, Moke said to him, gesturing with his head, hair to his shoulders, "Get in the back." He seemed stoned, half asleep, holding his left arm, the elbow, pressed in. He had on an old worn-out leather jacket zipped partway up, nothing under it but bare skin. Stick would bet he had a couple of tattoos on him somewhere, crude, threatening artwork.

"I got to get out," Stick said, "before you get in, don't I?" Wanting him to move back.

Moke said, "I guess if you're stupid."

Rainy was patting the inner side of his seat. "Through here, man. Just come through here."

Stick edged around between the seats to the rear compartment, hearing Moke say, "Where'd you find him at?" in that lazy, know-it-all tone so familiar, a twang of pure ignorance.

Moke climbed in and slammed the door. Then looked around at Stick. "Let me have the suitcase. Make sure you assholes aren't pulling any shit here."

The compartment bare, Stick was about to sit on the case. He got it up in front of him, kneeling on the carpet, and thought about shoving it hard into Moke's face. He could feel his heart beating.

Moke took the suitcase, laid it on his lap and fooled with the clasps until he got the top half raised. Rainy glanced out the side windows, then switched on the interior light. Stick raised up on his knees. He saw neat rows of banded one-hundred-dollar bills filling the suitcase. Moke picked up one of the packets and riffled through it, picked up another one, raising it to his ear and did it again. "Yep, it's all there." Rainy started to laugh. Moke half-turned to put dull eyes on Stick.

"The fuck you looking at?"

Rainy said, "Hey, where we suppose to go, man? Let's get the show on the road."

Stick got a good look at those sleepy eyes before Moke straightened around again, told Rainy to go on over to 87th Avenue and head south.

He could still feel his heart beating.

What he had to do was tell himself, keep telling himself, he had nothing to do with this, he was along

for the ride. Take a moment to think, realize where he
was now and not just react to things.

That guy he had read about last winter, the one who
wrote the book inside and they got him a parole, that
guy hadn't stopped to think. Maybe the other guy, the
guy working in the luncheonette who told him there
was no place for customers to go to the bathroom there,
the health department or something didn't allow it,
maybe he had said the wrong thing and the guy just
out had felt his heart beating. That was understand-
able. But out here you didn't use a knife on somebody
who said you couldn't take a leak. Inside you would
have pissed on the *guy*. But outside—he shouldn't have
even had the knife on him. He shouldn't have been *out*
to begin with after they knew he had killed inside and
didn't think anything of human life and after he had
spent all that time in the hole. They could've read the
guy's book and known they shouldn't ever let a guy like
that out. It was so different out... All the lights, for
one thing, all the headlights and streetlights, the neon
lights, all other people's lights that had nothing to do
with you. But inside you all lived together in the same
fluorescent light or lights in metal cages without shades.
You were in the same kind of light together all the
time. If a guy like Moke ever gave you that look or tried
to lean on you various ways, everybody was watching
and you better back him off or else sew up your asshole
because if you gave the guy the first inch he'd take the
rest any time he wanted.

You were lucky in there, Stick began to think. Jesus,
you were lucky. You know it?

He had backed some of them off, the hot-shit guys
in the wool-knit caps, but he wouldn't have backed them
off the whole seven years if he hadn't been lucky and
found a six-four, 240-pound soul-buddy by the name of
DeJohn Holmes. One moment thinking he was going
to die against the cement wall. The next moment
DeJohn's face grinning, showing him glints of gold and
a pink tongue, DeJohn saying, "Man, you my frien'.
Don't you know that?" Stick shaking his head, still
thinking he was going to die, and DeJohn saying, "Man,
I hear you the one did the motherfucker put me in here.

Tell me your pleasure, you want weed, you want shit, tell me what you want..."

Moke had been saying, "Turn here, hang a left the next corner," saying, "I got a Two-eighty Z'd put this fucker on the trailer in reverse." Saying, "About a Hunnert and fifteenth. It's before you get down to Montgomery..."

Now he said, "Past the school."

"I don't know where in the hell I'm at," Rainy said.

"Go on around the other side... Yeah, see the drive? In there."

Rainy said, "We going to school? I think it's closed."

They moved along the side of the old building, a playground or athletic field extending off to their left.

"Park along here," Moke said, "facing out. Turn your engine off."

"I can't see nothing," Rainy said.

They sat in silence.

"You got any weed?" Rainy said.

Moke didn't answer him.

"How about some music?" Rainy said. Then said, "Here comes somebody. Man, I hope it ain't cops."

Stick kneeled up. He saw headlights coming across the field toward them, creeping, coming out of darkness. In the beams now he saw a baseball diamond.

Moke said, "Pop your lights on and off...I said *off*, asshole!"

Stick remained quiet, watching as the headlights came to a stop maybe fifty or sixty feet away, along the third base line. The headlights went off. Then came on again glaring, switched to high beam.

Moke said, "Okay, get out," and watched as Rainy opened his door and stepped down. Moke shoved the suitcase at him. "Wait now. I want this boy to take it over," glancing around at Stick.

Rainy said, "Man, I got it, I'll take it. What's a difference?"

Moke said, "This boy here's suppose to take it's what I'm saying to you."

Rainy said, "No, man, I'm the one," backing away from the van with the suitcase.

Stick was looking at Moke's face, eyelids heavy in the light beams. He said, "Why would I do it? I come along for the ride."

He heard Rainy, outside, saying, "I'm going, okay? I want to say hi to Nestor. I haven't seen him."

Moke was shaking his head. "Jeez-us Christ—hey, come back here, will you!"

Stick saw interior lights go on as a door opened behind the headlights, giving shape to a full-size American car. A figure appeared at the right front fender. Rainy was in the beams now, out in front of the van. He called out, "Nestor? . . . Who is that?" Raised the suitcase in one hand and gave it a pat with the other. "I got it, man!"

Moke said, "Well, shit, I don't care."

All that was happening was there in front of Stick, watching from a second-row seat. He saw Moke's right hand dig inside the worn-out jacket.

Moke saying, "We'll make 'er a two-for-one special, today only."

Stick yelled out, "Rainy!"

Through the windshield he saw Rainy look back. Saw the figure by the headlights raise something in his hands and saw the muzzle flash as he heard the burst of gunfire, a hammering sound out in the open. Saw Rainy, outside, stumble and saw nickel-plate gleaming inside, the big revolver coming up in Moke's hand.

Stick lunged hard with his hands and shoulder into the back of Moke's seat and felt it rush on its tracks and stop dead and heard Moke's grunt as his head slammed against the windshield. Stick didn't wait, stop to look. The headlight beams lit up the compartment, showed him the rear-door latch. He banged through the doors and left the van running, digging hard, that hammering sound chasing him until he was around the corner of the school building.

With no idea of direction he walked residential streets of tile-roofed bungalows concealed in shrubbery, aroused a few relentless dogs, came out to commercial lights again, finding South Dixie Highway without knowing where it was. He waved down a taxi, let the driver look

him over, told the driver South Beach and didn't say
another word after that. They had to leave city streets
and traffic, break free onto MacArthur Causeway before he opened the window to feel the breeze coming off
the bay and to stare at distant solitary lights out in the
Atlantic ocean, listening in his mind to Moke saying,
This boy here's suppose to take it...

Suppose to die.

They sold nickel bags inside for seven bucks, they
sold regular cigarettes, shampoo, all that kind of stuff;
they sold shine made from potatoes, spud juice at ten
bucks a gallon, or let fruit juice stand till it turned and
drank that. Stick's former partner, Frank Ryan, died
of the potatoes in the prison hospital.

DeJohn Holmes said he could have anything he
wanted. A sateen jacket? Blue and gold with his name
on the back? *Stick*. Look nice, be a man of fashion.

Here was the strange part. It wasn't any of the colored guys in the wool-knit caps he had to watch.

No, out of five thousand eight hundred and something losers shuffling around, hanging out in the yard,
getting high, chasing sissies, it was a white guy named
Luther doing two to five who stared at him a few weeks,
circled in and finally told Stick he was going to kill
him. Why?

(Just like, why would he have thought he had to
watch Moke? He wasn't mixed up in that business.)

It didn't make sense: sitting there in the Big Top,
the dining hall, one morning with his cold scrambled
eggs and having this stone-eyed asshole biker chewing
with his mouth open telling him he was going to put a
shank in him when he least expected. The colored guys—
Christ, he got along fine with the colored guys and they
knew all about him, from DeJohn Holmes.

DeJohn was one of the "mayors" at Jackson and ran
a section of the yard, taking cuts on the card games
and numbers and renting out weight-lifting equipment
by the quarter hour when he wasn't using it. "Stay by
me when you need to," DeJohn told Stick. "I'll show
you how to jail, not lose any good time mixing up with
crazies."

But why did Luther want to kill him?

"'Cause he see you talking to me when you should be hanging out with the white boys. Start with that," DeJohn said. "Man like him, he don't even know how to brush his teeth. You watch him 'cause you don't know when the bug is going to go out on him and he turn hisself loose. Maybe he thinks in his stone mind you somebody else or you remind him of somebody stepped on him one time. Or he like to be like you and he can't. He say he going to shank you and you say watching the motherfucker eat is enough to turn you sick to death anyway. But see, he so slow in the head he has to think, man, to blink. So I get him assigned the meat shop and let him see he fuck with my frien' Stickley what can befall him."

Pure luck. Getting next to DeJohn, being discovered by him. DeJohn's story:

"A man point at me in Recorder's Court, City of Detroit, say yeah, that's him, that's him. Say I'm the one come in his place with a gun and cleaned out both his cash registers. Yeah, that's him. I draw thirty to life for the third and final time around. Now that man that pointed—not because I took his cash receipts but took his woman, *one* time, *one* night only and she love it—that man was Sportree, who died of gunshot at the hand of my frien' Ernest Stickley, Jr.," DeJohn said. "They some details missing, but it was some funny business following when you and Frank robbed the J. L. Hudson Company in downtown Detroit and got ate up."

Stick was careful. He said he was doing his time for a grocery store in Oakland County, not any homicide or robbery in downtown Detroit.

DeJohn said, "I know that. It's cool." He said, "Believe me, my man. You my man and it's cool. But it don't change you did Sportree and the dude was with him."

Stick said, to DeJohn only, okay, but it was unavoidable.

DeJohn said, "They all unavoidable when you have to do it. Like the two brothers in the shopping mall, in the parking lot, I believe was Northland."

Stick said yeah, that had been unavoidable too, the

two brothers wanting to *mug* him, for Christ sake, take his groceries.

DeJohn showed his gold and his pink tongue. "Groceries, yeah, shit"—enjoying it—"and the cash underneath the Wheaties from the store where you and Frank did your shopping." DeJohn said, "What they say, you could have got a hundred years just for the cars you used on those jobs. You take the fall on the grocery store, but they got Frank on the big one, didn't they? The Hudson's store."

Stick wondered how he knew all that.

DeJohn said, "You famous, baby."

When Luther made the move it was at a time when Stick was playing basketball in the yard. He left the game wheezing, out of shape, put on his work jacket and sat bent over on a bench trying to get his breath. He felt the wet on his back and thought at first it was sweat. He began to smell something . . . Christ, gasoline, and heard it when Luther dropped the match on him and *wouf* the back of his jacket went up in flames and he dove head-first over to land on his back on the cement and roll from side to side grinding in that hot sting . . . seeing the guy standing there with the Windex squirt bottle of clear liquid watching him.

DeJohn said it was the man's style and they should've known. "But the man lied to you, didn't he? Say he was going to shank you."

Three days later there was an accident in the butcher shop. Three witnesses in wool caps and white aprons swore Luther was splitting pork ribs with a cleaver, missed and cut off his left hand.

DeJohn said, "Man was lucky, wasn't he? He could have been seriously hurt and bled to death." He said, "I told him that, too."

There was all kinds of luck.

Stick sat on the cement porch of the Hotel Bon-Aire, listening to elderly people with New York Jewish accents complain about high prices, about Medicare and how Reagan had betrayed them. The hotel was light-green stucco, four stories, and seemed more like a retirement home than a hotel. Stick could feel the old

people staring at him; one asked if he was with the
government, looking things over.

August, no tourists, but still a lot of people on South
Beach.

He crossed the street always lined with cars and
went out on the sand past the clumps of sea grape and
the Cuban families cooking over charcoal, eating at the
picnic tables, and lay in the sun listening to bits of voice
sounds coming to him in Spanish. They sounded like
they were arguing but looked like they were having
fun. Try and figure out Cubans. He would lie in the sun
not moving and think about going up to Stuart or Day-
tona, or maybe over on the west coast around Naples,
work construction. He could always drive a transit-mix,
he'd done enough of that before.

With the hot glare pressing on his glasses and his
eyes closed tight he would try to look into the future
to a place where a man forty-two, starting over, could
find something interesting and make up for lost time.
If he was going to work he'd have to stay in Florida
and get back in construction. Not around Miami, though.
Or Detroit. People up there with seniority were drawing
unemployment. He didn't look so far ahead that he pictured himself an old man on the street, he pictured
himself *now;* but he couldn't, no matter how hard he
thought, see himself *doing* anything.

He still hadn't spoken to his ex-wife or his daughter.
Now, the way things were, he wasn't ready.

He was going to buy some clothes and get lucky
there. The manager of the hotel, an old bent-over guy,
showed him laundry packages of stuff a guy had left in
his room Stick could have for thirty bucks. Different-
colored shirts with little polo players on them, nice pants
just a little tight, a couple light jackets, everything
clean and neatly folded, fairly new stuff but without
that brand-new look, which Stick liked even better. The
manager said this young fella that left the clothes was
here in May, went off to Key West for the weekend and
never came back. The manager settled for twenty. Stick
went out and bought a pair of sneakers with blue stripes
on the sides.

They were the most comfortable shoes he'd ever

owned. In the early evening he'd walk up Collins Avenue from Seventh Street as far as Forty-first sometimes, up around the big hotels, and on the way back find a nice quiet bar, have a few bourbons over crushed ice, suck on that good stuff and feel himself, after a few evenings of it, beginning to settle down and get his confidence back. He burned the first day in the sun. But by the fourth day he looked like he was working construction again, getting tan faster than he ever had before. His hair even looked different, lighter; he let it fall in its natural bent instead of combing it back behind the ears. Four days and he looked like a regular Florida native. Next he would be going to discos, doing those slinky numbers with the ladies. There were enough of them around, he had a waitress or two hitting on him every night; but he wasn't anxious to move in that direction yet. He had to make up his mind about something, take one thing at a time.

He bought a post card to send to DeJohn that showed a bunch of alligators, one with its mouth wide open, next to a kidney-shaped cement pool. He would sit with his bourbon and stare at the empty white message side of the card, thinking:

> *Dear DeJohn, My luck almost ran out on me the other night...*
>
> *Dear DeJohn, man, could I use you right now...*
>
> *Dear DeJohn, Rainy asked me to go with him on a deal that was supposed to be a Sunday drive...*

But if he was going to go into all that, he'd have to put it in a letter. Tell what happened. Tell what he was going to do about it.

Well, the way it looked when he first started thinking about it, nothing.

Because there was nothing he *could* do. And because it was none of his business, it was Rainy's. Rainy knew there was always a risk, that kind of business, but it was how he made his living. It didn't matter what the deal was and it didn't do any good to think about it, because he didn't know all the facts.

Chucky owes a Cuban money. Chucky makes the payment. The Cuban takes the money—you assume that—and has Chucky's bagman killed. Why? Because as Rainy said, the Cuban was crazy, that's all. You were dealing with people, they weren't just weird, they had machine guns.

What he tried to do during the day, lying on the beach, taking walks along the surf, was think only about his future. Look at it in bright sunlight. Here it was, the world. What did it have to offer? All he had ever seen was one shady part of it. He found his thinking would come to: pick up a car and take off—and then his thinking would start jumping all over the place.

But, in the evening, settled down, feeling himself again, he was able to narrow his view, look at pieces of what had happened and come to a conclusion that had a hole in it but still made enough sense. He believed, first:

They didn't kill Rainy because he was Rainy. They didn't seem to care who they killed. Either one, he or Rainy would do. Moke said, "Shit, I don't care." Or both of them. Moke said, "Make it a two-for-one special."

But Rainy wasn't the first choice.

Stick could see Moke looking at him and saying, *"This boy here's suppose to take it."*

He had to squint hard trying to understand this part.

Maybe he'd heard it wrong. Or Moke had decided on his own to send him out there with the suitcase; so in Moke's mind he was *suppose to take it* and it was that simple.

Because if he'd heard it *right,* the way it sounded, then somebody had given Moke instructions. Send out the guy with Rainy. And who even knew there was going to be a guy with Rainy? Except Chucky.

So the second thing Stick came to believe:

Chucky was giving the Cuban somebody to kill. Part of doing business. Rainy said Chucky owned the Cuban money. Rainy didn't know he owed the Cuban a lot more than that, he owed the Cuban a life, too. Maybe Rainy didn't serve enough time to learn how those things worked. Stick knew.

He could sip his bourbon and know exactly why

Chucky had picked him. Because he had crossed the line, walked where he shouldn't have walked. Because he had given Chucky a look. Because he had inspected Chucky's home, a room in it, and said he wasn't impressed.

"You see anything you like?"

Asking for it. What was he supposed to say, yeah, I love it? Ask him who his decorator was?

Once Stick reached this conclusion he could look back at what had happened, including Rainy's murder, and accept it. He wished he could have helped Rainy. But Rainy and all these people were in the same life. It was how they dealt with one another. To them, inside or outside eighteen-foot walls with gun towers, the life was the same. So if in time Stick could put Jackson out of his mind he'd be able to forget about this business too. Begin by walking away from it.

Except that he began thinking about Chucky now and the one hole—a question mark, really—in his conclusion.

Chucky might have set them up, but a fact still remained. The suitcase tested by the four-hundred-pound gorilla had been delivered. Didn't Chucky owe somebody five thousand dollars?

On the post card with the alligators on it he sent to DeJohn, the message read:

Dear DeJ:

So far you aren't missing a thing not being here— as you can tell from that bunch of girls hanging around the swimming pool (over). Listen, I'd even take your old lady, Antoine, before I'd pick one of them. UGGGG!!! Tell the brothers disco is out and Soul is in. God bless you and take care of yourself. I'm going now to seek my fortune. Wish me luck.

Stick

He put on the lime green polo shirt, a pair of khakis faded almost white that didn't need a belt and matched the poplin jacket; he put on his new sneakers with the blue stripes and stuffed the rest of his new wardrobe

into a white canvas bag with blue handles. Well, look
at sporty, he said to the dresser mirror, liking his color
especially, his tan face smiling at him.

For seven years he had worn state clothes. He told
DeJohn, turning down offers of sateen athletic jackets
and sportshirts, he was reminding himself he was a con
and would not pretend to be something else until he
was out of there.

Now what was he?

He'd find out pretty soon.

SPLIT IMAGES

"Strong and true and persuasive, Leonard can
really write. He is astonishingly good."
John D. MacDonald

A Detroit homicide lieutenant and his beautiful
journalist lover track a rich, playboy killer and his
accomplice until tragedy strikes—and the
detective's duty becomes a relentless hunt for
revenge.

On Sale Now

The following excerpt is from Chapter 1...

In the winter of 1981 a multimillionaire by the name of Robinson Daniels shot a Haitian refugee who had broken into his home in Palm Beach. The Haitian had walked to the ocean from Belle Glade, fifty miles, to find work or a place to rob, to steal something he could sell. The Haitian's name was Louverture Damien.

The bullet fired from Robbie Daniels's Colt Python did not kill Louverture immediately. He was taken in shock to Good Samaritan where he lay in intensive care three days, a lung destroyed, plastic tubes coming out of his nose, his arms, his chest and his penis.

Louverture said he had an argument with the people who lived in the same room with him in Belle Glade. He paid forty dollars a week for the room and twenty dollars deposit for a key to the bathroom. But they had stopped up the toilet and it couldn't be used. They cleaned fish, he said, and threw the heads in the toilet. Speaking in a mixture of languages and sounds, Creole and Bahamian British English, he said, "I came here to search for my life."

The Palm Beach Police detective questioning Lou-

verture that evening in the hospital looked at him with
no expression and said, "You find it?"

Lying in the white sheets, Louverture Damien
was a stick figure made of Cordovan leather: he was
forty-one years old and weighed one hundred seventeen pounds the morning he visited the home on South
Ocean Boulevard and was shot.

Robbie Daniels was also forty-one. He had changed
clothes before the police arrived and at six o'clock in
the morning wore a lightweight navy blue cashmere
sweater over bare skin, the sleeves pushed up to his
elbows, colorless cotton trousers that clung to his hips
but were not tight around the waist. Standing outside
the house talking to the squad-car officer, the wind
coming off the ocean out of a misty dawn, he would slip
a hand beneath the sweater and move it over his skin,
idly, remembering, pointing with the other hand toward the swimming pool and patio where there were
yellow flowers and tables with yellow umbrellas.

"He came out. He crossed the yard toward the guest
house. Then, once he was in the trees over there I didn't
see him for, well, for a couple minutes. I started across.
Got about right here. Yeah, just about here. And he
was coming at me with a machete."

They could hear the high-low wail of the emergency
van streaking west on Southern Boulevard, a far-off
sound, fading.

As Mr. Daniels rubbed his bare skin the squad-car
officer would catch a glimpse of the man's navel cen-
tered on his flat belly, tan and trim, the cotton trousers
riding low, slim cut down to bare feet that were slender
and brown. The squad-car officer, twenty-seven years
old and in pretty good shape, felt heavy in his brown
and beige uniform, his gunbelt cinched tight to support
about ten pounds of police gear. He was from West Palm
and had never been in a millionaire's home before.

"Sir, you chased him out of the house?"

"No, I thought he was gone. I got the gun, came out
to have a look around.... I saw him coming out, I couldn't
believe it. He was still in the house when we got home."

The wind had been blowing for several days, the sky

overcast, an endless surf pounding in. Mr. Daniels said
he hadn't heard the man, it was more like he sensed
him coming across the yard, turned and there he was.

The squad-car officer wondered at first if Mr. Daniels
was a movie star. He had the features and that kind of
sandy brown curly hair some movie stars had and never
seemed to comb. The few lines in his face disappeared
when he opened his eyes that were pale blue and seemed
amazed in the telling of how he had actually shot a
man. Twice in the chest.

"Sir, how many rounds you fire?"

"I'm sorry—what?"

"How many times did you fire your gun?"

"Twice."

"What was he about, twenty feet away?"

"Closer. Ten feet maybe."

"Swinging the machete."

"What? Yes, raising it."

"But he didn't get a swipe at you."

"No."

Mr. Daniels seemed surprised, or else he seemed dazed
or preoccupied, thinking about it and the squad-car
officer's question would bring him back to now. Otherwise Mr. Daniels was polite and seemed anxious to be
of help.

People were always seeing movie stars around Palm
Beach and Mr. Daniels mentioned George Hamilton
twice. He mentioned Shelley Berman and he mentioned
Burt Reynolds. Mr. Daniels and some friends had gone
up to Jupiter to the Burt Reynolds Dinner Theatre, saw
"God's Favorite" and came back, had a few drinks at
Charley's Crab, then stopped by a friend's house to visit.
He said he got home at approximately four-thirty,
quarter to five.

Out visiting that time of the morning. The young
squad-car officer nodded. He had seen a young woman
down at the far end of the living room that was like a
hotel lobby. Younger than Mr. Daniels. Light brown
hair parted on the side, not too long; black turtleneck.
Eating an apple.

"Sir, your wife was with you?"

"She's in Aspen."

That stopped the yound squad-car officer. "Aspen?"

"Colorado. She's skiing. A houseguest was with me."

"Could I have that person's name?"

"Angela Nolan. Put down journalist. She's been interviewing me for a magazine, some kind of story."

"So she came in with you?"

"Yeah, but when I realized someone had broken in, the way the place was tossed, I told Miss Nolan, stay in the foyer and don't move."

The squad-car officer paused. One of Mr. Daniels's words surprised him, bothered him a little.

"Sir, you know what, if anything was taken?"

"No, you'll have to search the guy. I didn't touch him."

"How 'bout the help? Where were they?"

"The servants? They came out after."

"Must've heard the shots."

"I suppose so."

The young squad-car officer had a few more questions, but a detective arrived with the crime-scene people and the squad-car officer was sent out to South Ocean Boulevard to wave traffic past the police vehicles lining the road. Shit, what traffic? He was curious about a few things. He wondered if the houseguest, Angela Nolan, had seen any of the action. He wondered if Angela Nolan was staying in the main house or out in the guest house.

The young squad-car officer's name was Gary Hammond.

On the third day a woman who worked in a shirt factory in Hialeah and said she was Louverture Damien's wife came to Good Samaritan to sit at the man's bedside while he died.

Officer Gary Hammond was stationed outside the Haitian's hospital door now—in case the poor son of a bitch ripped out his tubes, somehow crawled out of bed and made a run for it. Gary would talk to the woman from time to time.

How come if she was married to Louverture she was living in Hialeah? To work, the woman said. Well, how come her husband didn't work there? The woman said

because her husband believed to work every day was a
bad thing. "If work was a good thing the rich would
have it all and not let you do it." Grinning then, showing her ugly teeth.

Jesus, the old broad was putting him on.

The woman was as skinny as the man in the bed.
An old leather stick with a turban and nine strands of
colored beads. She told Gary her husband had found
nothing in his life worthwhile. She told him her husband was sometimes a thief, but not a dangerous one.
He was too weak or cowardly to hurt anyone.

Gary said if he was harmless then what was he carrying the machete for, to get some coconuts?

The woman told him her husband had no *mashe*. She
said her husband run. The man say to him stop. Her
husband stop. The man say to him to come back with
his hands in the air. Her husband does this. The man
shoots him and *li tomber boum,* her husband falls with
a great crash.

Gary said, "You believe that?"

The Haitian woman said, "If he lie he could tell a
good lie, he can tell grand stories. But I don't know."
She said, "I go home tonight and fetch a white chicken
and kill it."

Gary said, "Yeah? Why you gonna do that?"

The woman said. "Because I'm hungry. I don't eat
nothing today coming here."

Gary said, "Oh."

He told the detective investigating the case the man
had died. The detective said, well, there were plenty
more where he came from. They stood between two
squad cars parked near the gate entrance to the estate.

Eyes half-closed in cigarette smoke the detective said,
"What do you think this place would sell for?"

Gary said he supposed about a million.

The detective said, "Try three and a half. You know
how many rooms are in that house? How many bedrooms?"

The young cop had a hard time figuring the house
out. It was classic sand-colored Spanish with a red-tile
roof, common enough in Florida, except it was big as a

monastery with wings and covered walks going out in different directions. Hard to make out because of all the vegetation: the shrubs and sea grape, royal palms, a hedge of hibiscus full of scarlet flowers hiding the wall that ran about three hundred feet along South Ocean Boulevard.

The detective said, "Six bedrooms up, four more in the guest house not counting the servants' wing. The place will sleep thirty without putting anybody on the couch."

How'd he know that?

"Authentic iron hardware on all the doors, you can pick any lock in the place with a screwdriver. It's got a sauna will hold about twenty naked bodies of either or both sexes."

The detective had been a Detroit cop before coming to Palm Beach. Middle-aged stocky guy with short arms that hung away from his body. That shitty-looking thin hair greased back in a shark-fin pompadour the young cop bet would hold for days without recombing. The guy sounded a little bit like Lawrence Welk, the way he talked, not so much with an accent, but seemed to say each word distinctly without running words together. He seemed dumb, squinting with the cigarette in his mouth to get a half-assed shrewd look. But the guy did know things.

The young cop was still wondering about the house-guest. Was she staying in the main house or the other one? He asked the detective if he'd talked to her. Angela Nolan.

Yeah, he had talked to her.

She corroborate what Mr. Daniels said?

The detective, with nineteen years Detroit Police experience, began to look at the young squad-car officer from West Palm a little closer, dumb-shrewd eyes narrowing.

Why?

Gary Hammond said he was curious, that's all. Was there something going on there? You know, hip-looking broad here, the guy's wife off skiing?

The detective said, "You mean you want to know do I think he's fucking her? Yeah, I think he's fucking her.

I think he'd be out of his fucking mind if he wasn't.
Robbie Daniels doesn't strike me as being double-gaited
or having any abnormal ideas what his dick is for," the
detective said. "I mean outside the popular abnormal
ideas that're getting more normal all the time."

Gary said he was just wondering.

The detective was not on the muscle. Sounding a
little sour was his everyday tone when he wasn't in-
tentionally kissing ass for information or some other
purpose. At those times he sounded appreciative, sometimes humble.

He said, "Did I ask him, you want to know, if he's
dicking her? No, I didn't. Did I ask if they're tooting
cocaine, maybe blowing a little weed? No, I didn't ask
him that either. The man comes home to his residence,
finds this Haitian in there in the dark. The Haitian
comes at him with a bolo or some fucking thing and
Daniels shoots him. Now, you want me to try and find
some holes in that? You want to implicate the broad,
the houseguest, like maybe she's in with the Haitian,
left the door open? Or how about we take a look, see if
Daniels has got any priors? That what you want?"

"Well, for one thing," the young cop said, "the Haitian told it different."

"I bet he did," the detective said. "I bet he said he
was fucking assaulted. You been out to Belle Glade
lately?"

"Sure."

"You see how they jungle-up out there, how they live,
you want to call it that? There's all kinds of work out
there. Every day five, six in the morning the buses are
waiting. No—this guy comes all the way from Belle
Glade, stops by four-thirty in the morning see if they
got any odd jobs, cut the grass or some fucking thing.
Comes strolling up to the guy with a machete and the
guy shoots him, you think something funny's going on."

Gary Hammond was patient. He was going to say
what was bothering him.

"He said something to me, Mr. Daniels. He said he
come in—he realized somebody was there from the way
the place was tossed."

"Yeah?..."

"He used the word *tossed*."

"So?"

"I don't know, it seemed weird. Like he used the word all the time, Mr. Daniels."

The detective said, "He say it was going down when he got home? How about, he looked at the guy but couldn't make him? TV—all that kind of shit come out of TV. They get to be household words. *Tossed*, for Christ sake."

"What about the Colt Python?"

"Cost him four and a half. I told him I could have got him a deal in Detroit."

"I mean is it registered?"

"Jesus Christ, get out of here, will you."

"Okay, but can I ask one more thing?"

"What?"

"Robbie Daniels—he isn't a movie star, is he?"

The detective said, "Jesus Christ, the man owns companies. He's got a big plant in Detroit supplies the auto industry with something or other. Has a development company owns land in seven states and down in the Caribbean islands. Resort hotels, condos, all that development shit. He's worth like in the neighborhood of a hundred million bucks—you want to know he's a fucking movie star."

The detective, wearing a light blue wash-and-wear suit over a dark blue sport shirt and a cream-colored tie, the open suit coat tight around his arms and shoulders, waited for the young squad-car officer to drive off before he buzzed for somebody to open the gate.

Mr. Daniels wanted to talk.

The detective had not been told this. He knew it the way he would know from a woman's glance in a bar there it was if he wanted any. The only difference here, he didn't know what Mr. Daniels had in mind. The detective had already gone down the list.

He isn't gonna ask you you want to play tennis or fucking polo, anything like that. Ask you you want to join the Seminole Club.

He isn't gonna ask you who your stockbroker is.

He isn't gonna waste his time, chitchat about this

and that. Though it would start that way.

What can you do he can't—outside of pressing two hundred ninety-five pounds straight up over your head? He thought about this following the drive that was lined with royal palms, but couldn't think of a good reason why the man would want to talk to him.

The detective's name was Walter Kouza.

"What's going to happen, not much at all," Walter Kouza said. "They'll run it past a grand jury, Palm Beach County Criminal Court. They have to do that in the case of a homicide. The jury will practically be instructed to call it justifiable and that's it."

"I have to appear, though," Robbie Daniels said.

"Yes, you have to appear, tell what happened. You're the only one knows, right? I take the stand, describe what the crime-scene people found—evidence of forcible entry, your gold cigarette lighter in the guy's pocket, Exhibit A, the machete—you'll be out in about twenty minutes."

There would be a silence and Mr. Daniels would nod to himself, getting it straight in his mind. The detective was surprised Mr. Daniels didn't act bored or like he was better than anybody else. He seemed like a nice down-to-earth fellow. Sat with a leg hooked over his chair. White cashmere today against his tan; faded jeans, gray and white Nike tennis shoes with the strings untied. The detective bet the guy never picked up his room when he was little or combed his hair. He still didn't.

He did kind of look like a movie star.

Or a cheerleader.

That was it. And the detective was the football coach. Big Ten. The two of them sitting around shooting the shit after the game. Only the coach called the cheerleader mister and maintained a pleasant expression.

Silence didn't bother the detective. He liked silence, waiting for the other fellow to speak. He liked the afternoon sunlight, the way it filtered through palm trees and filled the living-room-window wall twenty feet high. Sunlight made a silence seem longer because there was no way to hurry sunlight. You couldn't turn it off. He liked the cheerleader-coach idea too and thought of

Woody Hayes. Woody Hayes had probably never spoken to a cheerleader in his life outside of get the fuck out of the way. But this coach would talk to this cheerleader, yes *sir,* and wait until spoken to.

What he didn't like was not seeing an ashtray around anywhere, he was dying for a cigarette.

"Will there be any problem with the gun?"

"The one you used? No, I don't see a problem. I assume, Mr. Daniels, the gun's registered."

The cheerleader nodded again, thoughtful. "Yeah, that one is."

That one. The guy still nodding as the detective waited, in no hurry.

"Hey, listen, why don't we have a drink?"

"Fine," the detective said, "if you're going to have one."

He thought a servant would appear and they'd have to wait around for the servant to appear again with his silver tray. But the cheerleader jumped up—let's go—and led the detective through a back hall, up a narrow spiral stairway to an oval-shaped castle door Mr. Daniels had to unlock. Not the wrought-iron crap, Walter noticed, but Kwikset deadbolt double locks. The door creaked. Walter saw shafts of light in narrow casement windows, an oriental carpet, bigger than any he'd seen off a church altar, books from floor to ceiling, inlaid cabinets. Spooky, except for the oak bar and art posters that didn't make sense.

Walter said, "You must read a lot."

Robbie Daniels said, "When I'm not busy."

They drank Russian vodka on the rocks, Walter perched on a stool with arms, Daniels behind the bar—long-legged guy—one tennis shoe up on the stainless-steel sink. Hardly any sunlight now: track lighting, a soft beam directly above them and the rest of the room dim. Walter wanted a cigarette more than ever. There was a silver dish on the bar, but he didn't know if it was an ashtray.

He said, "Detroit, I had a bar down in the rec room, all knotty pine, had these ashtrays from different hotels, you know, different places."

"That's right," Robbie said. "I forgot, you're from Detroit."

"As a matter of fact born and raised in Hamtramck," Walter said. "Twenty-three sixteen Geimer. Went to St. Florian's, Kowalski Sausages right down the street if you know that area, or you happen to like kielbasa. Yeah, my old man worked at Dodge Main thirty-two years. You know they're tearing it down. GM's putting up a Cadillac assembly plant, buying all that land around there from the city. The city tells the residents, a lot of them these old people, what they're gonna give them for their houses, that's it, take a hike. Ralph Nader, you say GM to him he gets a hard-on, he's mixed up in it now... Yeah, technically I was born in Hamtramck, been a Polack all my life." Walter Kouza paused. His eyes, deep beneath his brows, showed a glimmer of anticipation.

"You know who lived not too far away? John Wojtylo." He waited. "The pope's cousin. Yeah, you know. John Paul the Second?"

"Is that right?" The cheerleader gave him an interested little grin.

"Yeah, the cousin use to work over to Chrysler Lynch Road. He was a sandblaster. Only the pope spells it different. Wojtyla. With a *a* on the end 'stead of a *o*. He's a Polack too. Hey, and how about that other Polack, Lech Walesa? He something? Doesn't take any shit from the communists."

Walter's blunt fingers brought a pack of Camels and a green Bic lighter from his shirt pocket. "And you live, your residence is in Grosse Pointe, if I'm not mistaken." He looked again at the silver dish on the bar; it was within reach.

The cheerleader was nodding, very agreeable. "Right, Grosse Pointe Farms."

"I could never keep those different Grosse Pointes straight. You live anywhere near Hank the Deuce?"

"Not far."

"There Fords all around there, uh?"

"A few. Henry, Bill, young Edsel now."

"They got, in the barber college right there on Campau near Holbrook? Heart of Hamtramck, they got a

chair Henry Ford sat in once, got his haircut. I don't
mean at the barber college, when the chair was someplace else."

"That's interesting," Robbie said. He took a drink
and said, "You mentioned the other day you were with
the Detroit Police."

"Nineteen years," Walter said. "Started out in the
Eleventh Precinct. Yeah, then I moved downtown,
worked Vice, Sex Crimes, Robbery..." Walter lighted
his Camel and pulled the silver dish over in front of
him. Fuck it. "It was never boring, I'll say that."

"You ever shoot anybody?"

"As a matter of fact I have," Walter said.

"How many?"

"I shot nine people," Walter said. "Eight colored guys,
one Caucasian. I never shot a woman."

"How many you kill?"

"I shot nine, I killed nine." Walter let himself grin
when he saw the cheerleader begin to smile, eating it
up.

"They were all DOA except this one guy, a jig, hung
on three hundred sixty-seven days, if you can believe
it. So technically his death wasn't scored as a hit. I
mean he didn't die of gunshot, he died of like kidney
failure or some fucking thing. But it was a nine-millimeter hollow nose, couple of them, put him in the
hospital, so...you be the judge."

"How about down here?" Robbie said.

"The guy was a quadriplegic, I mean when he died."

"Have you shot anyone down here?"

"In Palm Beach? I don't know if I tried to draw my
piece it would even come out. No, I haven't, but the
way things are going, all these fucking Cubans and
Haitians coming in here..." Walter stopped. "I got to
watch my language."

Robbie gave him a lazy shrug, relaxed.

Walter said, "Anyway, with the refugees coming in,
lot of them jerked out of prison down there in Cuba...I
know a gun shop in Miami I mentioned to you, guy's
got three outlets, he's selling five hundred thousand
bucks worth of handguns a *month*. Guy's making a fortune. He's got a range, he's teaching all these house-

wives come in how to fire three-fifty-sevens, forty-
fives...Can you see it? Broad's making cookies, she's
got this big fucking Mag stuck in her apron. But that's
what it's coming to. It didn't surprise me at all a man
of your position would have that Python. It's a very
beautiful weapon."

The cheerleader was pouring them a couple more.
"What do you carry?"

"Now? A Browning nine-millimeter." Walter laid his
cigarette on the silver dish, raised his hip from the stool
as he went in under his suit coat, pulled the weapon
from the clip-on holster that rode above his right cheek
and placed it on the bar, nickel plate and pearl grip
sparkling in the cone of overhead light.

"Nice," the cheerleader said.

"Detroit I packed a forty-four Mag and a thirty-eight
Smith Airweight with a two-inch barrel. But that's when
I was working STRESS. As a matter of fact, eight of
the guys I took out it was when I was with STRESS."

"I sorta remember that," Robbie said.

"Stop the Robberies, Enjoy Safe Streets."

"I'm not sure I ever knew what it meant."

"Yeah, Stop the Robberies...and so on. That was...let
me see, I was on it back in '72, '73. We'd go in teams
in a hot street-crime area, inner city. Dress like you
live around there. One guy's the decoy, the target. Stroll
down the street maybe act like you're drunk or you're
a john looking for some quiff. The other guys lay back,
see if you attract anything. See, we used teams of four.
That would be your decoy, your backup, he'd be like
another bum or civilian of some kind, then you'd have
two more guys in the car, they covered you. We cut
street crime way down, confiscated something like over
four hundred guns. We had to shoot some people to do
it but, well, it's up to them."

The cheerleader seemed to smile as he frowned, liking the idea but with reservations. "Isn't that entrap-
ment?"

Walter said, "Hey, they named the game. All we did,
we played it with 'em."

Robbie said, "May I?"

Walter said, "Sure." If the guy owned a Python he

could handle a Browning. He watched Daniels heft the
nickel-plated automatic, extending it now to take a
practice sight. But then looked up, lowering the gun.

A woman's voice said, "Don't shoot. I'll leave quietly."

Walter made a quarter turn on his stool.

The houseguest, Angela Nolan, stood in the oval
doorway. She was wearing a long navy blue coat with
her jeans, over what looked like a workshirt and a red
neckerchief. She said, "I'm on my way."

Robbie raised his eyebrows. "You're finished with
me?"

"No, but..." the girl paused. "Could I talk to you for
a minute?"

Robbie said, "Maybe some other time."

"I've got a plane. I just want to ask you something."

"Yeah...Go ahead."

"Could you come downstairs?"

"Not right now," Robbie said.

It was the girl's turn. Walter Kouza waited, feeling
something now, a tension that surprised him: the two
of them trying to sound polite, but with an edge, Mr.
Daniels's edge just a hint sharper than the girl's.

She said, "Thanks, Robbie, I'll see you."

He said, "Angie? Don't go away mad."

The doorway was empty. Walter swiveled back to
the bar as Robbie added, "As long as you go," and shook
his head, patient but weary.

Walter said, "Gee, she walks out—I thought you extended her every courtesy. She's a writer, uh?"

Robbie was fixing up their drinks.

"Suppose to be doing a piece for *Esquire,* part of a
book. At least that's what she told me. Like, 'The Quaint
Customs of the Rich' or some goddamn thing. She tells
me go ahead, do whatever I do, she'll *observe,* take some
pictures and we can talk later. Fine. I'm on the phone
most of the time I'm down here."

"I can imagine," Walter said.

"But then I sit down with her, she turns on her tape
recorder—you know what she asks me?"

Walter shook his head. "What?"

"What's it like to be rich? Am I happy? She goes from

that to, What do I think about abortion? What do I think about *busing* ... I couldn't believe it. Or, If you can have anything you want, what turns you on more than anything? Another one, related to that. If you have all the money you could possibly spend in a lifetime, why do you keep making more? I try to explain that the money itself is only a way of keeping score, but she doesn't understand that."

Walter didn't either.

"But then if I don't have time to sit down and talk, she gets pouty. I couldn't believe it. Really, like I'm taking up *her* time. She seems intelligent, you know, has some good credits, but when a broad comes on like it's the Inquisition and then gives you that pouty shit ... I said wait a minute. I agreed to be interviewed, yes, but you could get fucking washed out to sea tomorrow and I doubt anybody'd miss you."

"You told her that?"

"Why not? She came to me."

"Jesus, that's pretty nice stuff. I thought maybe she was like, you know, a girl friend."

Robbie said, "A girl friend? You look at her close? She's okay, but she's got to be thirty years old, at least. No, what she does, she gets you relaxed, talking off the cuff like she's your buddy, but what she's doing is setting you up. She's a ball buster," Robbie said. "I told her that. I said you don't care what I think. You interview somebody with a name, you just want to cut off his balls, make him look like a wimp. You know what she said? She said, 'I don't have to cut 'em, they come off in my hand.' I said well, not this pair, love. Go fondle somebody else."

Walter Kouza said, "Jesus." He never again thought of Mr. Daniels as a cheerleader.

CAT CHASER

"Elmore Leonard continues to dazzle us."
Cleveland Plain Dealer

An ex-marine takes a sentimental journey to
Santa Domingo, one of the world's choice
locations for intrigue, double-dealing and violence,
where he finds that chasing after a rich man's
money—or his wife—can be deadly.

On Sale Now

The following excerpt is from Chapter 4...

All over the world, Moran decided, the past was being wiped out by condominiums.

There were condos now on the polo grounds west of the hotel, where Amphibious Task Force helicopters had dropped off Marines from the U.S.S. *Boxer*, the grounds becoming a staging area for Marine patrols into the city. There were condos and office buildings rising in downtown Santo Domingo with the initials of political parties spray-painted on fresh cement, PRD and PQD; but only a few YANQUIS GO HOME now, on peeling walls out in the country, old graffiti Moran had noticed coming in from the airport.

There were young wives of ballplayers sunning themselves at the hotel pool—where the Marines had set up their water purification tanks—the young wives talking about housing and travel while their husbands, down here to play winter ball, took batting practice and went off for a round of golf.

There were no open fields near the hotel now. The gardens were gone, where the first group of Marines had dug in. The Kentucky Fried Chicken place on the corner of Avenida Washington and Socorro Sanchez was gone. The mahogany trees on the street south of the U.S. embassy were still there; the trees looked the same.

They had gone up this street beneath the arch of trees, wide-eyed in the dark, all the way to Nicolas Penson in a war where the street signs were intact and they found their way with a Texaco road map. In the morning they saw people in the streets, crowds of people lining Washington along the oceanfront, like they were watching a parade. They were—waving at the tanks and amtracs. Even with the FUERA YANQUIS signs painted on houses most of the people seemed glad to see them.

The next day, filing back to the embassy, a Marine walking point was shot dead by a sniper; Item Company, at Checkpoint Charlie north of the embassy, drew heavy fire and soon there were snipers working the whole neighborhood, what was supposed to be the International Safety Zone, using bazookas as well as small arms, even old water-cooled 30s that pounded out a heavy sound and at first were thought to be .50-caliber. The Marines moved crosstown, east, establishing a Line of Communication with the Eighty-second Airborne troopers coming into the city across the Duarte Bridge. The LOC held the rebels cornered in the old section of the city and kept the loyalists from getting at them. But it didn't stop the snipers.

A battalion officer told them, "You got your friendlies and you got your Unfriendlies." He told them most of the snipers were hoodlums, street gangs who'd armed themselves when the rebels passed out guns the first day. These people were called *tigres* but were not trained or organized, not your regular-army rebels. The *tigres* were out for thrills, playing guns with real ones. "So don't fire unless you're fired on." That was a standing order.

Wait a minute. You mean there're *rules?* Somebody said, "We're *here,* man." Two Marine battalions and four Airborne. "Why don't we go downtown and fucking get it done?"

The question was never answered. By the end of the first month of occupation nineteen U.S. military had been killed in action, one hundred eleven wounded.

Moran said to his driver today, in the early evening sixteen years later, "I have a friend who was here with the Eighty-second, the paratroopers. He believes we could have gone into the rebel area, the old section, and ended the whole thing in about fifteen minutes."

"Yes, I believe it, too," the driver said.

"You were here?"

"Yes, I always be here."

"What side were you on?"

"This side." The driver, who was an old black man with Indian cheekbones that looked as though they had been polished, tapped his steering wheel. "Three taxicabs ago, the same Number Twenty-four. Chevrolet, but not new like this one." They were in a '76 Chevrolet Impala, Moran in front with the driver, the windows open, Moran now and again smelling wood smoke and the smell would take him back to that time.

"You were glad to see the Marines?"

"Yes, of course. To have peace. I drove pressmens from the United States. Yes, we come to a corner, a street there, we have to go fast or those rebel fellas shoot at you. One time the bullets come in this side where you are, they hit here"—he slapped the dashboard—"and go out this way past me, out the window." The driver's name was Bienvenido. He was born in 1904 and used to Marines from the United States. He said to Moran, "You want to see where Trujillo was killed, yes?"

"Tomorrow," Moran said.

"And the old quarter, Independence Park."

"Tomorrow," Moran said. He was silent a moment and then said, "Do you know a woman by the name of Luci Palma?"

The driver thought about it and shook his head. "No, I don't think so. Luci Palma..."

They followed the drive into the grounds of the Hotel Embajador, past the front lawn where the American civilians had waited with their luggage to be evacuated. Moran said, "Will you do something for me?"

"Yes, of course."

Moran took a piece of notepaper from his shirt pocket

and unfolded it. "I want this message put in the newspaper. In *Listin Diario* or *El Caribe,* I don't care, whichever one you like better. All right? Tell them to put it in a box. You know what I mean? With lines around it. So it'll stand out. Okay?"

"Yes, okay."

"In English."

"Yes, in English."

"Just the way it's written here. Okay? See if you can read it." He handed Bienvenido the piece of notepaper with the hand-printed message on it that said:

CAT CHASER

> is looking for the girl who once
> ran over rooftops and tried to kill
> him. Call the Hotel Embajador.
> Room 537.

Moran waited for the driver to ask him a question. Bienvenido stared at the notepaper, nodding, his lips moving.

"You understand it?"

"You want a girl to call you?"

"The girl I met when I was here, before."

"Yes."

"She'll recognize 'Cat Chaser.' If she sees it."

"Yes."

"That was the code name for my platoon. When I was here. I was Cat Chaser Four, but she'll know who it is. I mean if she's still here." It didn't seem enough of an explanation and he said, "This girl shot at me, she tried to kill me. I don't mean it was anything personal, it was during the war. Then, I was taken prisoner by the rebels and I got a chance to meet her...You understand what I'm saying?"

Bienvenido was nodding again. "Yes, I understand. You want this girl. But if you don't find this girl, you want another girl?"

Mary de Boya watched Moran enter the lobby. She watched him pick up his key at the desk and cross to the elevators. She was aware of an instant stir of excitement and in her mind, concentrating hard, she said, *Look this way*. She said, *Moran, come on. Quick. Look this way!*

The elevator door closed behind him; he was gone.

Maybe she was expecting too much. It was dark in the hotel cocktail lounge. Even if he'd looked over he might not have been able to see her. Or their telepathy was rusty.

A few years ago Mary de Boya could stare across the lounge at Leucadendra and make Moran feel her eyes and look at her. Moran could do the same. In the dining room or the club grill she would feel it. Raise her eyes to meet his and something would pass between them. Not a signal, an awareness. They could smile at each other without smiling. Raise eyebrows, almost imperceptibly, and make mutual judgments. Aloud they could make comments removed from reality that would whiz past her husband, his wife, and they would know things about each other that had nothing to do with their backgrounds, both from the same city. That was a coincidence, nothing more. Though it was handy if needed, when Andres drilled her with his secret-police look and wanted to know what they'd been talking about. "Detroit." When in fact they'd been talking about nothing in particular, nothing intimate, nothing sane, for that matter, "Detroit" was the safe answer. "We just found out both of our dads worked at Ford Rouge, but George lived on the northwest side and I lived downriver, in Southgate." The look between them had remained harmless. Still, each knew it was there if they wanted to make something of it.

Mary smiled thinking about it now, realizing she missed him.

It didn't seem possible to miss someone you saw only once or twice a week over a period of a few years; but she had continued to picture him and think about him and what she felt now was real. You know when you miss someone.

Before today she hadn't seen Moran since his divorce. Since his father-in-law drummed him out of the club, ripped the crest from his blazer. Mary saw it that way in fantasy, in flashes: Moran standing at attention in his beard and sneakers, expelled for refusing to wear white patent-leather loafers with tassels, and matching white belt. Out. Refusing to talk about real estate, grain futures, tax shelters, more real estate. Out.

She should have jumped up and yelled and run across the lobby. Nine hundred miles from home...

Call his room.

An outfielder with the Cincinnati Reds' Triple-A farm team came over to where Mary sat at the first table inside the lounge and asked if she'd have a drink with him. Good-looking, well built, at least ten years younger than she was. Mary smiled and said, "I'd love to. Sit down."

Giving her something to do, so she wouldn't have to make an instant decision. For all she knew Moran was meeting someone, a girl...

They talked about the World Series in New York and Guerrero, the L.A. Dominican, hitting the home run Sunday, the outfielder telling how everybody in the lounge watching it on TV had practically freaked out, their boy coming through. She flirted with the outfielder a little, because she could see he was taken with her and it made her feel good. The mysterious American woman in expensive casual silk, alone in Santo Domingo. The muscular, curly-haired outfielder sat with his big shoulders hunched over the table eating peanuts one at a time, holding back.

Mary de Boya, at thirty-four, was quite likely the best-looking woman the outfielder had ever seen in real life. Her blond honey-streaked hair fell in soft waves to her shoulders framing delicate features, a fine mist of freckles, startling brown eyes.

She asked the outfielder what it was like to stand at the plate and see a hardball coming at you at ninety miles an hour. The outfielder said it didn't matter how fast it came, you had to stand in there, you couldn't give the pitcher nothing. He said it was the curveballs that were more apt to do you in. Curves low and away. The outfielder asked Mary if she had ever been down here before. She told him a few times, for polo matches at Casa de Campo. He said oh, was that what she was

down for this time? Mary paused. She said no, she was
meeting her lover. The outfielder said oh...

"Now I've got to run," Mary said, and left the outfielder half in, half out of his chair. At the front desk
she asked for Mr. Moran's room number.

The clerk said, "Mr. Moran," and looked it up. "Five
three seven."

"How long is he staying?"

The clerk had to look it up again. "The twenty-ninth.
Four days."

Mary turned part way, paused and turned back to
the desk again. "I think I'd like a room."

"Yes," the clerk said, "we have a very nice room. Or
we have a suite if you like a sitting room, too."

"That's fine," Mary said, though she didn't seem quite
sure about something. "I don't have my luggage with
me." She looked at the clerk now for help. "It's at Casa
de Campo. If I give them a call, can you send someone
to pick it up?"

"Yes, but it's seventy miles there," the clerk said. "I
don't know how rapidly they can do it."

"Do the best you can," Mary said. She filled out the
registration card using her maiden mame, Mary De-
laney, and an address in Miami Beach off the top of her
head, committing herself now, beginning to make her
move, thinking: If you're meeting someone, Moran, I'll
kill her.

The view from Moran's room was south, past the swimming pool area directly below and down an abrupt grade
to a postcard shot of white colonial buildings and palm
trees on the edge of the Caribbean. In this time when
dusk was becoming night, color gone from the sky, he
could hear voices, words in clear Spanish and bikes
whining like lawnmowers: the same distinct, faraway
sounds they listened to sixteen years ago in tents on
the polo fields. The sounds of people doing what they
did despite the other sounds that would come suddenly,
the mortar and rocket explosions, five klicks removed
from the everyday sounds, off somewhere in the city of
Santo Domingo. He didn't like those first days, not
trusting the people, not having a feel for the terrain.

He studied his Texaco map by flashlight and memorized names of the main streets, drew red circles for checkpoints, Charlie and Delta, the embassy, the Dominican Presidential Palace, the National Police Barracks. Take Bolivar to Independence Park, where burned-out cars blocked intersections, and duck. Beyond this point you could get killed. He liked it once he had a perimeter and was able to tell his fire team what they were doing. None of them had been to war.

He would walk those streets tomorrow...and hear the voices again on the field radio..."Cat Chaser Four, you read? Where the fuck are you?"...And the girl's voice coming in. "I know where you are. I see you, Cat Chaser...Hey, Cat Chaser, come find me...You no good with *tigres*. All you know how to hunt, you Marines, is pussy. Come find me, Cat Chaser Four, whatever your name is...This is Luci signing off."

Luci Palma, the sixteen-year-old girl who gave them fits with an M-1 carbine from World War Two. The girl who ran over rooftops...

The room-service waiter came with a bucket of ice that held three bottles of El Presidente beer. Moran signed, gave the waiter a peso and said, "Were you here during the revolution?"

The waiter didn't seem to understand.

"Hace dieciséis años," Moran said.

"Oh, yes, I was here."

"What side were you on?"

Again the waiter hesitated.

"Que lado? Los generales o los rebeldes?"

"No, I don't fight," the waiter said. "I like peace."

"No one I've talked to was in the war, the *guerra*," Moran said. "I wonder who was doing all the shooting."

The phone rang.

"I was in Samaná," the waiter said.

"Everybody was in Samaná," Moran said. "Thanks." He walked behind the waiter going to the door and stopped by the nightstand next to the bed. As the phone rang for the fourth time he picked it up.

"Hello."

The voice instantly familiar said, "Moran? What're you doing in Santo Domingo?"

He said, "I don't believe it. Come on..." grinning, sitting down on the bed. "What're you doing here?"

"I asked you first."

"Where are you?"

"About twenty feet above you. Seven thirty-five."

"I don't believe it." He sat up straight and wanted to make his voice sound natural, casual, as he said, "Mary?... Is Andres with you?"

"He can't come back here, George. He's afraid somebody'll shoot him."

"Gee, that's too bad. I mean that you couldn't bring him." He heard her giggle. "Well, who're you with?"

"Nobody. I'm all alone."

"Come on...I don't believe it."

"Why're you so amazed?"

"You kidding? I don't believe *this*. I'm not sure I could even imagine something like this happening."

She said, "Are you alone?"

"Yeah, all by myself."

"I mean, are you meeting anyone?"

"No, I'm alone. Jesus Christ, am I alone. I don't believe it," Moran said, getting up, having to move around now, excited. "You know I recognized your voice right away? What're you doing here?"

"I saw you in the lobby. A little while ago."

"Yeah?..."

"If you're not busy, you think we could have a drink?"

"If I'm not *busy*? Even if I was... Listen, I've got three cold bottles of El Presidente sitting right in front of me, unopened."

She said, "Why don't you come up and see me, George? Bring your beer with you."

"Right now?"

"I'll have the door open."

She did, too.

Waited just inside the sitting room for him so that when he appeared in the doorway and entered the short hallway past the bathroom and closet he would have to come to her and she would open her arms.... Except that he was carrying the ice bucket in front of him with both hands and when she raised her arms he didn't know what to do and they stood there staring at each other, anxious, aching, until she said, "Make up your mind, Moran. Are you going to hold the beer or me?"

He hurried past her into the sitting room, placed his bucket on the coffee table next to hers that held a bottle of champagne. Now they could do it. Now as he turned she came into his arms like it was the most natural thing in the world, wanting to hold and feel each other close after only looking at one another for all those years and keeping a distance between them, sometimes inches, but always a distance. There. It felt good, better than imagined, and from that moment something more than two old friends meeting. Their mouths came together, unplanned, but this too seemed natural, their mouths seeking, brushing, fitting softly as their bodies relaxed and began to blend....

Abruptly, without a flicker, the lights in the room and in the hall went out.

They pulled slightly apart, still holding each other. Moran said very quietly, "We must've blown a fuse. Generated too much electricity."

"I'd believe it," Mary said, "if I hadn't been here before. They run low on power and have to black out parts of the city."

"For how long?"

"I think fifteen or twenty minutes. Didn't you notice a candle in your room?"

"No...Where you going?"

"To find the candle. I saw it somewhere..."

"I can't see you."

"I think it's in the bedroom."

He followed the sound of her voice, moving carefully now in total darkness, hands ready in front of him. His shin hit the coffee table and he heard the ice bucket rattle against glass.

"Where are you?"

"I'm in the bedroom," Mary said. "I think."

He moved in that direction, around the coffee table, and came to a doorway that seemed darker than the dark sitting room. Entering cautiously, a room he'd never seen, with nothing to picture from memory, Moran extended his arms like a man sleepwalking. He caught the scent of her perfume, moved a cautious step and felt her hair brush his face. She was between his arms and he closed them around her now, feeling her hands slide up over his ribs.

He said in almost a whisper, "You find the candle?"

"No. It must be in the bathroom."

He said, "Do we need it?"

He felt her hands, her breath—this slim girl, not as tall as he'd remembered her, the image of her across a room. He felt the silky material covering her bare skin, the skin smoothly taut, her body delicate but firm pressing into him, their mouths brushing, finding the right place again, and this time drifting into a dreamlike kind of consciousness, Moran aware but not seeing himself, Mary moving against him, moving him, guiding gently, and Moran knew where they were going, feeling the foot of the bed against his leg and it was all the bearings he needed. They bailed out in the dark and fell into the double bed in the excitement of each other. She said, "You don't know how long..." He said, "I know." Barely moving their mouths apart to speak. She said, "God, I want you." He said, "How do you get this off?" He said, "Shit, I tore it." She said, "I don't care, tear it," pulling his belt apart. He said, "Can you wait, just a second?" She said, "No." He said, "I can't either. Jesus." She said, "Don't talk." He said, "One second...," and got on his knees and pulled off her sandals and slacks and somehow got out of his pants, pausing then, catching his breath to pull his shirt over his head and when he sank down again into the bed they were naked, with nothing to make them hold back all that longing they could now release. The lights came on as they were making love, a soft bedroom glow that was just enough and could have been cued as Moran said, "Oh, man," and had to smile as he saw Mary smiling. Now they could see each other and it wasn't simply an act of their bodies, they were identified to each other, finally where they wanted to be more than anywhere. Moran's urge raised him stiff-armed, raised his face to the headboard, to the wall above them and he groaned, letting go that was like, "Gaiii-yaaa!" and brought Mary's eyes open, but she closed them again, murmuring, moving, and remained in iridescent sparkling dark as he came back to her again, winding down, settling.

She felt moisture on his back, his shoulders. She said, "Oh, God," as though it might be her last breath. Then opened her eyes to study his face in repose, his eyelashes, his eyelids lightly closed.

She said quietly, "Well...how have you been?"

"Not too bad."

"Do you always do that?" Her words a soft murmur.

"What?"

"I thought you were in pain."

"I was, sort of."

"You really throw yourself into it."

"That was the first time I ever heard myself do that. It just came, so to speak." He opened his eyes. "You do an analysis after?"

"No, but I've always wondered about you," Mary said. "Do you know how many words we've spoken to each other, counting today?"

"We didn't have to use words. That was the spooky part about it. I always had the feeling we knew each other when we were little. Little kids who played together, then didn't see each other for about thirty years."

"I'm not that old."

"You're old enough. You know what I mean," Moran said. "I don't have to explain anything to you."

"No."

"Boy, you are really something."

She said, "There's more to it than that, isn't there?"

"There's way more," Moran said. "I don't mean just in bed. Will you tell me what you're doing here?"

"I came down with some girls from the club. Polo buffs. Or that's their excuse to get away and party, maybe play a little tennis. Actually they came down yesterday, but I couldn't make it till today."

Moran said, "Yeah, I ran into them at the airport. They looked sort of familiar—one of 'em's name is Philly?"

"Right, Philly, Marilyn and Liz, my old tennis court buddies."

Moran said, "You're staying here, this place? I don't think it's very *in*."

"No, what happened," Mary said, "my friends drove in from Casa de Campo to meet me and go to a cocktail party at the Santo Domingo Country Club. Mostly embassy people."

"Yeah?..."

"Then I was supposed to drive back to Casa de Campo with them later. The polo matches start tomorrow." Mary paused. "But I left the party."

"Why'd you come here?"

"Well, you told Philly you were staying here..."

"Yeah?..."

"I thought I'd stop by and say hi."

Moran said, "Really?" And began to smile. "You came to the hotel just to see me?"

"You want the truth?" Mary said. "I came to Santo Domingo just to see you."

"But you said—"

"I lied," Mary said. "I didn't plan to make the trip. But then Philly called last night to coax me, tell me about the embassy party and happened to mention she saw you at the airport." She said, "There, I've bared my soul to you, Moran."

"It's a nice one," Moran said, "I'm getting excited all over again. But what about the polo matches?"

"I think polo's boring," Mary said. She smiled and he smiled. "I sent for my bags. For the time being I don't have any clothes."

Moran said, "You don't, huh?" Still smiling.

CITY PRIMEVAL
High Noon in Detroit

"The action is so devious and the dialogue so convincing, one can hardly turn the pages fast enough...Elmore Leonard, already the best suspense writer in America, gets better with every book." <u>Miami Herald</u>

On the trail of a psychotic killer, a Detroit cop who believes in old-fashioned justice finds himself up against a deadly choice: uphold the law or bring down the killer in a more expedient way.

They let Clement sit alone in the interrogation/file room for about forty minutes before Wendell Robinson went in to talk to him.

It was close to 10:00 P.M. Raymond Cruz crossed his feet on the corner of his desk and closed his eyes to the fluorescent lights...while Hunter made coffee and told about Pamela and the rough time Pamela was having trying to make it with all the goddamn amateurs out there giving it away, selling themselves for Amaretto on the rocks, Kahlua and cream...Raymond half listening, catching glimpses of the Carolyn Wilder he had never seen before this evening, wondering what Clement had said to her, wondering if—at another time, the right time—she'd be easy to talk to.

The windowless file room, about seven-by-eleven, held three folding chairs, an old office table and a wall of built-in shelves where closed case-records were stored. On the wall directly behind Clement was a stain, a formless smudge, where several thousand heads had rested, off and on, during interrogations.

Wendell said, "How well you know Edison?"

Clement grinned. "Detroit Edison?"

"Thomas Edison."

"I never did understand nigger humor," Clement said.

"Man whose car you were driving this evening."

"That's his name? I just call him Tom. Only nigger I ever knew owned a Chevy. He loaned it to me."

"He a friend of yours?"

"Friend of a friend."

"I understand he's a doorman. Works over at 1300 Lafayette. That where your friend live?"

"I forget which friend it was's a friend of old Tom's."

"Sandy Stanton lives over there," Wendell said. "She's a pretty good friend, isn't she?"

"You know everything, what're you asking me for?"

"She a friend of yours?"

"I know her."

"She loan you the Buick last night?"

"It tickles me," Clement said, "you people trying to act like you know something. You don't have shit, else I'd be over'n the Wayne County jail waiting on my exam."

"We want to be ugly, we could get you some time over there right now," Wendell said. "Driving after your license was revoked on a D.U.I.L., that's a pretty heavy charge."

"What, the drunk-driving thing? Jesus Christ," Clement said, "you trying to threaten me with a fucking *traffic* violation?"

"No, the violation's nothing to a man of your experience," Wendell said. "I was thinking of how you'd be over there with all them niggers."

"Why is that?" Clement said. "Are niggers the only ones fuck up in this town? Or they picking on you? I was a nigger I wouldn't put up with it."

"Yeah, what would you do?"

"Move. All this town is is one big Niggerville with a few whites sprinkled in, some of 'em going with each other. You'd think you'd see more mongrelization, ex-

cept I guess they're just fucking each other and not
making any kids like they did back in the plantation
days...You want to know something?"

"What's that?"

"One of my best friend's a nigger."

"Yeah, what's his name?"

"You don't know him."

"I might. You know us niggers sticks together."

"Bullshit. Saturday night you kill each other."

"I'm curious. What's the man's name?"

"Alvin Guy." Clement grinned.

"Is that right? You knew him?"

Clement said, "Shit, I could tell you anything,
couldn't I?"

"There was a window in there I'd have thought seriously about throwing him out," Wendell said, and
Raymond nodded.

"I know what you mean."

"Man doesn't give you anything to hook onto. You
understand what I'm saying? He jive you around with
all this bullshit, you don't know who's asking who the
question. See, he does the judge, then he goes home to
his bed. We been up two days and a night."

"Go on home," Raymond said.

"I'll stay on it, you want me to."

"We'll let the old pro take a shot," Raymond said,
looking over at Hunter. "The old reddish-gray wolf. What
do you say? If we can't shake him tonight we'll turn
him loose, try some other time."

Hunter got up from his desk. He said, "You want to
watch, see how it's done?"

There was no clear reason why Hunter was the
squad's star interrogator: why suspects so often con-
fided in him and why the confessions he elicited almost
always stood up in court. Maureen said it was because
the bad guys got the feeling he was one of them. Hunter
said it was because he was patient, understanding, sym-
pathetic, alert, never raised his voice...and would cite
as an example the time last winter he questioned the

suspect, young guy, who admitted "sort of strangling"
two women while "overcome with cocaine." The young
guy said he thought this belt one of them had was a
snake and wanted to see what it would look like around
their necks; that's how the whole thing had come about,
while they were sitting on the floor tooting and having
a few drinks. But he refused to tell what he did with
their bodies. Hunter said, well, the bodies would show
up by spring, when the snow melted, and added. "Unless
you're some kind of animal and you stored them away
for the winter." Hunter noticed the suspect appeared
visibly agitated by this off-hand remark and quickly
followed up on it, asking the suspect if he liked animals
or if he was afraid of them or if he related to animals
in some way. The suspect insisted he hated animals,
rats especially, and that when he went out to the aban-
doned farmhouse a few days after and saw that rats
had been "nibbling" on the two women he immediately
took measures to prevent them from being "all eaten
up." He cut the bodies up with a hacksaw and burned
them in the coal furnace. He was no animal...

"What you do," Hunter said, "you see your opening
and you step in. You don't let the guy out until he's
told you something."

"Remember this room?" Hunter asked Clement.

"Yeah, I remember it. I remember you, too."

"Still put grease on your hair?"

"No, I like the dry look now," Clement said.

"Good," Hunter said. "You messed up the wall the
last time—all that guck you slicked your hair down
with."

Clement looked over his shoulder at the wall. "Don't
you ever clean this place up?"

"We hose it out once a week," Hunter said, "like at
the zoo. Get rid of the stink."

"What're you," Clement said, "the heavy? First the
nigger and then you. When's the good guy come in?"

"I'm the good guy," Hunter said. "I'm as good as it's
gonna get."

"You haven't read me my rights."

"I figured you know it by heart. You want me to read 'em to you? Sure, I'll read 'em."

Hunter went out into the squad room. Raymond Cruz sat at his desk with his eyes closed. Hunter poured himself a mug of coffee, picked up a *Constitutional Rights* form and went back into the file room, sat down and read the first paragraph of the document to Clement.

"You know your rights now? Okay, sign here." Hunter pushed the document over to Clement with a ballpoint pen.

"What if I don't want to sign?"

"I don't give a shit if you sign or you don't sign. I'll put down you refused, gave us a hard time."

"But why do I need to sign it?"

"I just told you, asshole, you don't."

"I'm in here for questioning as . . . what?"

"You were arrested."

"For not having a driver's license? What's this got to do with it?"

"While in custody the defendant's record was examined with reason to believe he might be involved in a homicide under investigation and was detained for questioning."

"Detained—I can hear you," Clement said. "And then my lawyer stands up and says, 'Your Honor, this poor boy was held against his will, without any complaint being filed and was not read his rights as a citizen.' Buddy, I don't even know why I'm here. I mean, nobody's told me nothing yet."

"You're in here, Clement, because you're in some deep shit, that's why."

"Yeah? Friend of mind was in this room one time, he refused to sign and nothing happened to him."

Hunter said, "Look at it from the court's point of view, Clement, all right? . . . Which looks better, we get a warrant and arrest you for first degree murder, which carries mandatory life? Or, we report you came to us voluntarily to make a statement. Under no duress or apprehension you describe the circumstances—"

Clement began to smile.

"—under which a man lost his life, telling it in your

own words, putting in whatever mitigating factors there may be, such as your mental or emotional state at the time, whether there was some form of incitement or threat to your well being...what're you grinning at?"

"You must think I went to about the fifth grade," Clement said, "buy that load of shit. I don't have to say a word to you. On the other hand I can say anything I want and you can't use it because I ain't signed your piece of paper. So what're we sitting here for?"

"It's a formality," Hunter said. "I got to give you the opportunity to make a statement. You don't, then I take you down the garage, stand you against the wall and beat the shit out of you with the front end of a squad car."

Hunter said to Raymond Cruz, "Fuck—we don't get him with the piece, we don't get him."

"He sign the sheet?"

"No, but what difference does it make? He's not gonna say anything. He knows the routine better'n we do."

"I'll give it a try," Raymond said, "Go on home."

"No, I'll stick around."

"Go on. What're we doing, we're just chatting with the guy."

"Clement...how you doing?"

"You're in trouble," Clement said. "Carolyn told you, you guys don't talk to me without her."

Raymond said, "You spend the night here, she might be a little mad when she finds out, stamp her feet maybe. But she knows it's part of the business. We see a shot, we have to take it. Listen...let's go in the other room. You want some coffee?"

Clement said, "I wondered who the good guy was gonna be."

He sat at Hunter's desk swivelling around in the chair, unimpressed, until he spotted the mug-shot display, the 263 color shots mounted on the wall and extending from Norb Bryl's desk—where Raymond sat sideways to the coatrack by the door. Raymond sat side-

ways to the desk facing Mansell, ten feet away, who
was turned sideways to Hunter's desk.

"Poor fuckers," Clement said. "You put all those people away?"

"About ninety-eight percent of 'em," Raymond said.
"That's this year's graduates, so far."

"About ninety-eight percent niggers," Clement said.
"The fuck am I doing sitting here?"

"You want me to tell you?" Raymond said.

"I wish somebody would," Clement said. "I can guess
what your heart's desire is, but I *know* you don't have
nothing good else I'd be across the street."

"I might've jumped the gun a little."

"I believe you jumped the hell out of her."

"You know how you get anxious."

"Got to stay cool," Clement said. "Evidently you got
somebody made a car somewhere—"

"At the scene, for one."

"Yeah?" Non-committal.

"And at the Hazel Park track," Raymond said. "The
car belongs to Del Weems, a friend of Sandy Stanton."

"Yeah?"

"She's staying at Del Weems' apartment, using his
car sometimes."

"Yeah?"

"So are you. I know I can place you over at 1300
Lafayette if I talk to enough people. And there's a good
chance I can put you in the car at Hazel Park, the same
time the judge was there, same night he was killed."
Raymond looked at the wall clock. "About twenty-two
hours ago...What did you think when we got on you
this fast?"

"You got a tape recorder going some place?"

Raymond raised his hands, helpless. "For what?"

"Won't do you any good if you have." Clement looked
up at the ceiling and raised his voice as he said, "You
can't use anything I'm saying, so fuck you!"

"I can hear you fine," Raymond said pleasantly. "I'm
not trying to pull anything, legal or otherwise. I just
thought you and I might save some time if we know
where we stand."

"That sounds like it makes sense," Clement said, "except I think it's pure bullshit. There's no way I can be doing myself any good sitting here. This is a miserable fucking place, you know it?"

"You never went before Guy, did you?"

"No, I was never in his court."

"So it couldn't be anything personal."

"Jesus, you got your mind made up, haven't you?"

"The only other reason I can think of, somebody must've paid you." Raymond waited. Clement didn't say anything. Raymond smiled slightly. "That person finds out you're in custody I think it would clutch him up some...the kind of situation you get into when two or more people are involved in a murder. Like the guy that was shot in front of the Soup Kitchen, the promoter. You remember him? This past summer. Who was convicted? The shooter. Not the guy that arranged it. He copped and we gave him immunity."

"Jesus Christ," Clement said, "you're starting to sound like that other chicken-fat dick, giving me this scary story like I got grits or something for brains."

"I guess I ought to come right out with it," Raymond said.

Clement nodded. "I think you'd feel better."

"Okay," Raymond said, "what's gonna happen as soon as we put you in the Buick—we already have the Buick at the scene—you'll want to start talking deal. You'll give us something if we'll ease up a little. Except by then it will probably be too late. We settle for Clement Mansell, he gets the mandatory, that's it. Did somebody pay him? Who knows? Or more to the point, who cares? See, there isn't that much wrath, you might say, or righteous indignation involved. Some people think the guy who did the judge ought to get a medal instead of a prison term. But it's a capital crime, so we have to go through the motions. I want you to understand now we *will* nail you down, there isn't any doubt about that...*unless,* before we put in all these hours and get pissed off and cranky and unreasonable...you say okay, here's what happened, here's the name of the guy that put up the fee...*then* we could probably do something for you. Talk to the prosecutor about second degree, maybe even get it down to manslaughter and put the mandatory on the guy that hired you. You see what I mean?"

Clement leaned his right forearm on the desk and stared across the ten feet at Raymond Cruz.

"You got a nice, polite way about you. But underneath all that shit, you really want my ass, don't you?"

"I don't have a choice," Raymond said.

"You feel this as something personal? I mean this particular case?"

Raymond thought a moment; he shrugged.

"Shit no," Clement said. "What's bothering you, three year ago you guys blew it. You had me convicted on a triple, air-tight with witnesses, and I walked. That's been bothering the shit out of you. So now you're gonna try and get me on this one to make up for it. See, now it *does* get personal. Right? You don't care who hit the judge, you just want *me*. Am I right or wrong?"

Raymond took his time. He said, "See, we're finding out where we stand."

"Am I right or wrong?"

"Well, I have to admit there's some truth in what you say."

"I knew it," Clement said. "You got no higher motive'n I do, you talk about laying things on the table, see where we stand. You don't set out to uphold the law any more'n I set out to break it. What happens, we get in a situation like this and then me and you start playing a game. You try and catch me and I try and keep from getting caught and still make a living. You follow me? We're over here in this life playing and we don't even give a shit if anybody's watching us or not or if anybody gets hurt. We got our own rules and words we use and everything else. You got numbers, all these chicken-fat dicks that'd rather play the game than work; but I got the law to protect me and all I got to do is keep my mouth shut, don't associate with stupid people and there's no way in hell you're gonna lay this one on me...or any of the others."

Raymond nodded, thoughtful but at ease, alert but

not showing it. He said, "You know what, Clement? I think you're right." There was a silence. "What others?"

And again, a silence.

Clement leaned on his arm that rested along the edge of the desk, as if to draw a little closer to Raymond Cruz.

"You know how many people I've killed?"

"Five," Raymond said.

"Nine," Clement said.

"In Detroit?"

"Not all in De-troit. One in Oklahoma, one in Kansas."

"Seven in Detroit?"

"That's right. But five—no six of 'em was niggers."

"Counting Judge Guy."

"Count who you want, I ain't giving you a scorecard lineup."

"When you were with the Wrecking Crew, huh?"

"Most by myself. Well, kind of by myself. Other fella didn't do shit."

"Going into dope houses, huh?"

Clement didn't answer.

"Like the one on St. Marys, the triple?"

Clement didn't say anything.

"I don't mean to pry," Raymond said. "You arouse my curiosity." He sat back in Norb Bryl's stiff swivel chair and placed his legs on the corner of the desk. "It's interesting what you said, like it's a game. Cops and robbers. A different life that's got nothing to do with anybody else."

"Less we need 'em," Clement said. "Then you get into victims and witnesses. Use who you can."

"But what it comes down to," Raymond said, "what it's all about, I mean, is just you and me, huh?"

"That's it, partner."

"Some other time—I mean a long time ago, we might have settled this between us. I mean if we each took the situation personally."

"Or if we thought it'd be fun," Clement said. "You married?"

It took Raymond by surprise. "I was."

"You got a family? Kids?"

"No."

"So you get bored, don't have nothing to do and you put more time in on the job."

Raymond didn't say anything. He waited, looking at the wall clock. It was 11:15.

Clement said, "You ever shoot anybody?"

"Well ... not lately."

"Come on, how many?"

"Two," Raymond said.

"Niggers?"

He felt self-conscious. "When I was in Robbery."

"Use that little dick gun? ... I been meaning to ask why you put the rubber bands around the grip."

"Keep it from slipping down."

"Cheap fuck, get a holster. Shit, get a regular size weapon first, 'stead of that little parlor gun."

"It does the job," Raymond said. It sounded familiar: a table of cops at the Athens Bar drinking beer.

Clement said, "Yeah?" and let his gaze move around the squad room before returning to Raymond Cruz, sitting with his feet on the desk. "Say you're pretty good with it, huh?"

Raymond shrugged. "I qualify every year."

"Yeah?" Clement paused, staring at Raymond now. "Be something we had us a shooting match, wouldn't it?"

"I know a range out in Royal Oak," Raymond said. "It's in the basement of a hardware store."

"I'm not talking about any range," Clement said, staring at Raymond. "I was thinking out on the street." He paused for effect. "Like when you least expect."

"I'll ask my inspector," Raymond said, "see if it's okay."

"You won't do nothing of the kind," Clement said, "cause you know I'm not kidding."

They stared at each other in silence and Raymond wondered if this was part of the game: who would look away first. A little kids' game except it was real, it was happening.

He said, "Can I ask you a question?"

"Like what?"

"Why'd you shoot Guy?"

"Jesus Christ," Clement said, "we been talking all this time, I think we're getting some place—what difference does it make why? Me and you, we're sitting here looking at each other, sizing each other up—aren't we? What's it got to do with Guy, or anything else?"

52 PICK-UP

"A tightly-wound thriller with a smash-up climax."
The Village Voice

This is a fast-paced and chilling tale of a Detroit businessman who discovers he is the player in a ruthless game of sex and blackmail in which the only way to win is murder.

On Sale Now

The following excerpt is from Chapter 11…

Mitchell was in the kitchen when he heard the front door open. He hadn't eaten. He had been here more than two hours, sitting in the den most of the time, waiting for her, wherever she was. He was in the kitchen deciding if he should make a sandwich, wondering if it would be all right. It was his house, but now he didn't live here. It gave him a strange feeling. With the sound he moved away from the refrigerator. Looking at an angle through the doorway, past a corner of the dining room to the foyer, he saw Barbara, her hand on the partly open door. He heard a man's voice, outside, say, "We'll make it again real soon, okay?" But he didn't place the voice until Barbara closed the door and turned and saw him. Mitchell said to himself, Ross. God Almighty, Ross. Already. He saw the look on her face. Surprise? Caught? Caught in the act. Or momentarily startled. When she came into the kitchen her expression was calm, composed.

"How long have you been here?"

"A little while. Not long."

"I went out for dinner."

"I thought you might've. Where'd you go?"

73

"The Inn," Barbara said. "I think it's going downhill. Getting noisy."

Mitchell nodded. "Very popular I hear with unescorted ladies."

"I wasn't alone."

"I know you weren't."

There was a silence. They were standing only a few feet apart, looking at each other, waiting. It was in Mitchell's mind that he was going to stand there and not say anything as long as it took to outwait her. But the stubborn feeling passed. She looked good. In black, with pearls. She looked better than ever. She had been out to dinner with Ross. He knew it. But if she didn't want to tell him about it, if she wanted to keep him hanging—she had every right to turn and walk away if she wanted to. He felt dumb. A big dumb jealous husband putting his wife on the spot.

He said, "I was thinking about making a sandwich. Is that all right?"

She waited a moment, her eyes still holding his. "I don't know. I'll have to ask my lawyer."

"Have you hired one?"

"For God sake, we haven't even *talked*." She put her purse on the counter and moved past him to the refrigerator. "I have no idea what's going on in your head and you ask me if I've hired a lawyer." Opening the refrigerator she looked at him again. "What kind of a sandwich do you want?"

"I don't care. Anything."

"Hot dog?"

"That's fine."

"Just tell me one thing, all right? Are we talking about a divorce?"

"Barbara—I don't know. I don't know what you're thinking either. The little bit we've talked, I probably haven't made much sense."

"Not a hell of a lot. Do you want a beer?"

"All right."

He watched her go into the regrigerator and move a pitcher of orange juice to reach the beer. As she handed him the can Barbara said, "Are you going with the girl or not?"

"No."

"What does that mean? No, not at the moment, or no, you're not seeing her anymore?"

"Barbara, she's dead."

She waited, her hand holding the refrigerator door open. "You mean she died? Something happened to her and she died?"

Mitchell wasn't sure why he told her. It came out of him. She was dead and he had to say she was dead. He couldn't pretend she was a girl from another time who had moved away or dropped out of sight. She was dead.

He put the beer can on the counter and took the photograph out of his coat pocket and showed it to Barbara. He didn't say anything. He held it up to her and watched her face.

Barbara turned from the refrigerator, letting the door swing all the way open.

"Is that the girl?"

"No, a friend of hers. It's the man I'm interested in. Have you ever seen him before?"

Barbara took the picture from him to study it and he felt his hope die. There was no hint of recognition on her face. She said, "No, I don't think so."

"It's not the man who was here, with the accounting service?"

"Definitely not. He was skinny and his hair was longer."

"I was hoping," Mitchell said. "Well..." He took the picture from her and dropped it on the counter.

"Mitch, who are they?"

"They work at a model studio. I was there today. I had a feeling, I don't know why, and I took their picture."

"They're friends of yours," Barbara said, "or what? Why were you there?—a model studio." There were so many questions she wanted to ask him, that she wanted to know, *now,* and he stood quietly looking down at the photograph, staring at it with his calm closed-mouth expression. "Mitch, will you please, for God sake, tell me what's going on!"

Behind her, the bright inside light of the refrigerator showed milk cartons and the pitcher of orange juice, cans of beer, jars, packages wrapped in butcher's paper, dishes covered with silver foil.

"I want to tell you," Mitchell said. "But it doesn't have anything to do with you. It's happening to me; I don't want to see you involved in it."

"Mitch—whatever it is—it's happening to *us*. I'm already involved. As long as I'm your wife I'm involved."

He looked at her, not saying anything. He walked over to her and slowly, carefully, put his hand on her shoulder. As she looked up at him he reached around her to push the refrigerator door closed.

"All right," Mitchell said. "Let's sit down."

There were four cigarette stubs in the ashtray. A drink, half-finished, was forgotten, the ice melted. Barbara sat across the coffee table from him, sitting forward in the low chair. During the past half hour she had not taken her eyes off him.

"But what if she isn't dead?"

"I know she is."

"You see people shot in the movies. It can look real—"

"I thought of that," Mitchell said. "She's dead. I saw her face. Her eyes were open, with a look I've never seen before. She wasn't breathing. She wasn't faking it, she was dead."

"What would they do with her? Where do you keep a dead body?"

"I don't know. Maybe they buried her somewhere."

"With your gun and your coat."

"My fingerprints are on the gun. My permit—"

"*If* they kept her body," Barbara said. "If they still have it, or know they can get it."

"That's their whole point," Mitchell said. "I pay, or they tell the police where to find her."

"All right, what if you go to the police and tell them first?"

"Tell them what?"

"The whole thing," Barbara said. "I mean you wouldn't be going to them if you actually did it. They'd realize that."

"I don't know where the girl is. I can't prove anything."

"At least you could tell them exactly what you saw. Then it's up to them to investigate and find out who did it."

"How?"

"I don't know. It's what they do."

Mitchell thought for a moment and came at it from another angle. "Let's say there are suspects, they're arrested. Let's say they actually did it. Do you think they're going to implicate themselves, tell the police where to find the girl's body?"

"Then look at it this way," Barbara said. "If they saw the possibility, that it might happen—the whole thing blow up in their faces—then they wouldn't have kept the girl's body."

"They haven't necessarily kept it. It's probably hidden somewhere."

Barbara shook her head. "If there's the least possibility they could be tied in with the murder, they don't want a body around that could be found by someone, accidentally discovered, and used to implicate them. Mitch, why would they take the chance?"

"You're saying they got rid of her. Put her somewhere she can't be found."

"I think so," Barbara said. "They say if you refuse to pay, they tell the police. That could have been a bluff. They frighten you enough and you pay off. If you don't they have nothing to lose. So if they didn't get rid of her body before, they would the moment they see the police beginning to close in."

"Then nothing can be proved."

"Go to the police and tell them. Let them worry about it."

"Barbara, once it's told—you don't edge into something like this. I tell them a girl's been murdered, it's out, everybody knows about it. It's in the papers, the whole story. I'm fooling around with a young girl and she ends up dead."

"Can't it be approached, you know, confidentially? Keep it quiet?"

"I don't see how. Not when someone's been killed."

She stared at him a moment. "You're afraid of the publicity? Is that what's bothering you?"

"Barbara, the girl died because of me, because I knew her. That bothers me more than anything. The publicity—" He paused. "I don't see this, if it got in the papers, as what you'd call bad publicity. I see it as something that could destroy our lives, affect our kids, ruin, wipe out everything I've worked for, built up. Listen, I feel this more than I can explain to you. I mean I want to do what's right, I want to see them caught. But I'm also realistic, practical about it."

"I told Ross," Barbara said, "I thought you were sometimes cold-blooded. But that isn't really the word."

"Use it if you want," Mitchell said. "I'm saying I don't feel, my conscience doesn't tell me I have to go to the police. Like that's the only way."

"But what other way is there?"

Mitchell paused. "What if—I don't know how—I handled it myself?"

"Mitch, please. Don't say that. They've already killed someone."

"So have I. With six machine guns."

"Mitch, that was different. My God, I don't have to tell you that."

"I'm not saying I'm going to. I'm saying what if."

Barbara stood up. "Mitch, look, if there isn't a body, you can refuse to pay them. If there's nothing they can hold over you—the threat of telling the police—then you're out of it. There isn't a thing they can do."

"But they'd still be loose," Mitchell said. "They killed that girl as coldly as you can do it, and they'd still be loose." He looked up at his wife. "I'm in this, Barbara. I'm not going to run, I'm not going to try and forget about it and hope it goes away. I'm going to do something."

That was exactly what she was afraid of.

Barbara made him an omelet with cheese and onion and green pepper. He stood at the counter to eat it, with French bread and an avocado, and the beer she had handed him earlier. He was tired, but he didn't feel like sitting down. He was thinking about Leo Frank and picked up the photograph again. He was thinking about getting in the car and driving down to Detroit. It would take him about twenty-five minutes, that's all. Start with Leo, because he still had a feeling about Leo. Walk into the model studio and this time talk to him. Lead him with questions and watch his reaction.

Barbara said, "Did you tell them you'd pay?"

Mitchell shook his head. "No."

"Do they think you will?"

"I don't know."

"Mitch, even if you wanted to pay them"—she paused as he looked up at her—"where would you get the money? Over a hundred thousand dollars?"

"I've never considered paying, so I haven't thought about it."

"We don't have that kind of money. Do they think you just keep it in the bank?"

"Barbara, I don't know what they think. I guess they figure I can get it if I have to, at least ten thousand bucks at a time. The first payment's due tomorrow."

"And another one a week from tomorrow," Barbara said, "and another a week later. Can you put your hands on thirty thousand dollars that fast?"

"I could if I had to."

"You'd have to sell some stock, wouldn't you?"

"Or borrow it from the bank."

"But without borrowing—you can't touch the trust funds, can you?"

"No. Or the depreciation investments. In fact, I just sold most of our fooling-around stock last month and put the money into five-year municipal notes. We can't touch that either."

"So if you wanted to pay them off," Barbara said, "how much do you think you could raise?"

"If I had to?" Mitchell paused. "I don't know, maybe forty or fifty thousand without too much trouble."

"Do you think they'd settle for that?"

"Are we just thinking out loud or what?"

"You said the one sounded as though he knew as much about you as your accountant."

"He knows about the royalty. That's enough."

"What if you showed him exactly how much you can

pay?" Barbara said. "Whatever the amount is, but that's it and no more. Do you think he'd settle for it?"

Mitchell put his fork down. He looked at his wife, at her drawn fixed expression, and knew she was serious. "You think I'd make a deal with them?"

"Mitch, they *killed* that girl. If you won't go to the police then you have to pay them. Don't you see that? Or they'll kill *you*."

"You think if I pay them, that's all there is to it? They go away, we never hear from them again?"

"Talk to them when they call," Barbara said. "Tell them you'll show them facts and figures, what you can afford to pay. If you can convince them that's it, why wouldn't they take it?"

"You make it sound easy," Mitchell said. "Expensive, but easy."

"How much is your life worth?" Her voice was calm; the concern, the fear, was in her eyes.

"I don't know, if I got close enough to talk to one of them," Mitchell said, "I'm liable to break his jaw."

Barbara closed her eyes and opened them. "Mitch, go to the police. Will you please?"

He finished the beer in his glass and placed it on the counter. "Talk to one of them," Mitchell said then. "Not all of them. Just one."

"What do you mean?"

"That could have possibilities," Mitchell said. He nodded, thinking about it. Yes, it sure could. Get one of them alone and talk to him. If he could first find out who they were.

"What are you talking about?"

"Nothing really. Maybe an idea; I don't know."

"Would you like some coffee?"

"No thanks. I want a bed more than anything else." He looked at her for a moment, saw no response in her eyes and started to turn away.

"Mitch—"

There it was, a good sound. Soft, familiar. He turned to look at her again.

"What?"

"God, I miss you."

"I miss you too."

"Then don't go," Barbara said. "Stay here."

"I'm sorry." He wasn't sure how to say it, but he knew he was going to try. "I'm really sorry I hurt you. I don't know why—it was a dumb thing I got into."

"I know." Barbara nodded slowly. "Let's not talk about it anymore, all right? Let's go to bed."

UNKNOWN MAN NO. 89

"Remarkably ingenious...will keep you on the edge of your chair." <u>The New York Times</u>

When a process-server with the reputation for being able to find anyone is hired to track down a missing criminal in Detroit, he learns that big money makes people do dangerous things—and finds himself caught in a treacherous labyrinth of deception, betrayal and murder.

On Sale Now

The following excerpt is from Chapter 10...

"Snowing," Mr. Perez said. "Nearly the middle of April, it's still snowing."

"It's just flurries," Ryan said. "That kind of snow, it doesn't stick to the ground at all. It's a wet snow."

"I remember, coming in from the airport there was still some snow, very dirty-looking snow, patches of it along the highway, with all the rain you've had." Mr. Perez stood in the alcove of the floor-to-ceiling window looking out at the gray mass of sky and the light snow swirling in the wind. "You certainly have a long winter," he said.

"Or you can look at it as kind of an asshole spring," Ryan said. He didn't believe it—sitting here talking about the weather. "It's great for the skiers, though. Up north, I heard on the radio, they've still got a fifteen-to twenty-inch base," Ryan said—if the guy really wanted to talk about it.

Maybe he was finished. Mr. Perez came away from the window and sank into his favorite chair—the Spanish governor of a colony, member of an old, titled family, who'd been sent out here and was pissed off about it, but kept it locked up inside. Ryan was here to give his report.

He was sitting on the couch this time instead of a straight chair, figuring they would have quite a bit to discuss. It was one-thirty in the afternoon. Near the door was a room-service table pushed out of the way. So Mr. Perez had eaten his noon dinner. Everything on the menu, it looked like, the way the table was cluttered with dishes, empty wineglasses, those silver dish covers and messed-up napkins. The man had a noon dinner, he had a dinner. He still seemed too skinny to be a big eater. Or else the white shirt, the collar, was a couple sizes too large.

"You find out he's colored," Mr. Perez said. "How does that change anything?"

"Didn't you think he was white?"

Mr. Perez nodded. "Yeah, I guess I did, judging from his name. It wasn't Amos Washington or...Thurgood Marshall, one of those. But now Mr. Leary's deceased and we know he has a wife. What's her name?"

"Denise. Denise Leann. But she goes by Lee."

"And you talked to her."

"Yeah, but not knowing, as I mentioned, she was his wife. The way I got it, she was like an ex-girlfriend."

"An ex-something, huh? Well, now we contact the wife, who we'll presume is his legal heir, and deal with her. You say she's gone. But she doesn't have any reason to hide, does she?"

"Not that I know of."

"And you know what she looks like."

"Uh-huh."

"So you shouldn't have any trouble locating her. Do you see a problem?"

"There's a couple of things," Ryan said. "More than a couple. Something I didn't tell you. He's black, but the wife, Lee, is white."

"Up here, I'm not too surprised," Mr. Perez said.

"The other thing, she's an alcoholic."

Mr. Perez thought about that a moment.

"I like alcoholics. I've had a few. They're very easy to deal with, very cooperative. What kind of an alcoholic is she?"

"What do you mean, what kind? What does she drink?"

"I mean, how far along is she? Does she work? Or does she sit home and hide bottles around the house?"

"I don't think she works. No, she couldn't. But it's not that kind of a setup either, hiding bottles. They're right there on the sink."

"See," Mr. Perez said, "a white woman marries some-body like Robert Leary, what we've learned about him, she's pretty hard up, scraping bottom. A woman like that, her nose stuck in the bottle, no income, she's going to take anything she can get."

Ryan kept quiet. He'd listen and let the man tell him about alcoholics, what they were like.

"We make an offer, this kind of deal, the alcoholic woman isn't going to see money, unh-unh. She's going to see visions of gin bottles dancing in her head. She'll sign the agreement in blood if she has to."

"She's a wine drinker," Ryan said.

"Cheap dago red, huh?"

"Chilled Sauterne."

He could see the dirty glass on the bar and the empty half-gallon jugs in her kitchen. He realized he was trying to upgrade her and he didn't know why.

"The other thing, or one more to add to it," Ryan said, "the police are looking for her, too."

Mr. Perez raised his eyebrows. "They suspect she might've killed him?"

"Well, they'll question her, there's no doubt about that," Ryan said. "As my friend was saying, it's a homi-cide and they'll give it the full treatment. It doesn't matter, the fact they're glad the guy's dead. Somebody killed him and it's their job to find out who."

"You have any ideas about that? You seemed to've been getting in there pretty close," Mr. Perez said.

"Well, I ran into a guy, yes, and I know he found out where Leary was staying. The same night it happened, in fact. This guy, I don't know what his name is, knows Leary's wife. I told the police about it already, gave them a half-assed description of the guy—his clothes, his hat, you know—but I don't know what's going to come of that. What I started to say—they're looking for his wife, yes, but mainly so she can claim the body, get it out of the way."

"And you say they don't know where she is."

"No, but I think it's only a matter of time," Ryan said. "They go looking for somebody, the cops, they find them. They've already checked the hospitals. She hasn't been admitted anywhere."

"Checked the *hos*pitals?" Mr. Perez said. "Check the bars, you say she's an alcoholic."

"Well, see, she's in pretty bad shape."

Ryan heard the toilet flush and paused. He looked over at the closed door that led to the bedroom. Mr. Perez waited, not offering an explanation.

A woman, Ryan thought. He wondered if she'd come out. He said, "I think his wife might've finally realized she was in trouble and it could kill her if she kept drinking. Her calling me like that was a good sign."

"So maybe she'll call you again," Mr. Perez said. "Save you some work."

"That'd be fine. But now I've got a feeling she's still drinking. She had a couple this morning to straighten her out and they went down so good she kept going. So then she might've gotten another room somewhere. She could call me, sometime, but I'll probably have to wait till she bottoms out again." Ryan shook his head. "It's very tough, trying to quit like that."

He saw Mr. Perez's gaze move past him. Ryan glanced over at the doorway to the bedroom.

A stringy, heavy-boned farmer-looking guy had opened the door and was coming out, his head down, buckling his belt.

Ryan looked back at Mr. Perez, who was watching the man with a relaxed, pleasant expression. Mr. Perez said, "I hope you had a good one, Raymond. You were in there a half hour."

"Traveling," the man said. "It throws me off my schedule. I sure don't like to go on the airplane."

"Raymond Gidre," Mr. Perez said. "Shake hands with Mr. Ryan, fella I was telling you about."

"Yes-sir, it's a pleasure to meet you." Raymond Gidre smiled cordially, reaching for Ryan's hand as he rose. The man seemed eager, flashing perfect dentures in a weathered face that had been recently shaved and bore traces of talcum powder. His curly black hair, combed back severely, plastered down, glistened with tonic that Ryan could smell and recalled from barbershops years before. Lucky Tiger. The man had a small-town-barbershop look about him. Like he'd just come out of one. He wore a short-sleeved sport shirt. Ryan noticed the tattoo on his right forearm—something black and red—but didn't want to stare at it. He shook Raymond Gidre's hand and nodded and said he was glad to meet him, held for a moment by the dentures and the pale eyes smiling. Just a good-natured back-country boy—stringy and hard after a half-dozen years on a Louisiana prison farm.

"Raymond here's visiting from a place near New Iberia, Louisiana," Mr. Perez said. "Avery Island, huh, Raymond? Where the hot sauce comes from."

"Home of Tabasco," Raymond said. "Yes-sir," walking over to the room-service table. He poked through the napkins and silver lids, found a hard roll, and bit into it, still poking around. "You didn't eat your snapbeans."

"Finish 'em up," Mr. Perez said, and looked at Ryan again. "Raymond works for me on and off in special capacities, you might say. For instance, if we see you need some help, Raymond's the boy for it."

Ryan nodded as though he knew what Mr. Perez was talking about, then decided he might as well ask.

"What kind of help?"

"Well, if you were to need protection of one kind or another, somebody to see you don't get hurt. I wouldn't want that to happen."

"I wouldn't either," Ryan said. "But what would I need protection from? I'm looking for the wife now. The bad guy's dead."

"That's true," Mr. Perez said, "but somebody killed the bad guy, didn't he? Somebody, you said yourself, found out where he was staying. By the way, this man you talked to last night, was he colored?"

Ryan nodded.

Mr. Perez looked past him, across the room. "Got a colored boy, Raymond, might want to give us trouble."

"It's all the same to me," Raymond said, eating from a plate of green beans, "I'm not prejudice."

What the hell was going on? Ryan felt himself starting to get a little worked up. Perez talked to him very seriously, then would say something to his hired hand and almost break out in a giggle.

"I don't understand something," Ryan said. "We don't know who the guy is, the black guy I met. We don't know if he was the one that killed Leary. I mean, we can't even begin to assume something like that. Or, okay, let's say even if he *did,* what's it got to do with me? That I'd need protection? I'm looking for the *wife.*"

"You said you put a notice in the paper—"

"I also put another one in," Ryan said, "that's due to run tomorrow."

"Let me finish," Mr. Perez said. "All right?" He waited a moment, staring at Ryan with his solemn expression. "You put a notice in the paper and two people called you up. Is that correct?"

Now he was standing on the carpet, in the principal's office. "That's right," Ryan said.

"You thought one of the two might have been Leary, but not both of them."

"That's right," Ryan said.

"You suspected somebody was looking for him."

"I *knew* that. And it's obvious somebody found him. The guy's dead." Ryan paused a moment. Mr. Perez's tone might be a little pissy, but maybe he was sincere, at least meant well. "I see," Ryan said. "You think if it was the guy I met in the apartment, he might be afraid I'll identify him."

"That type of thing," Mr. Perez said. "I didn't have anything that specific in mind, of course, when I telephoned Raymond and asked him if he'd like to visit the Motor City. I felt we were mixing with ugly people, getting ready to do business with one of them; so it wouldn't hurt to have some protection. Mr. Leary's dead, but there are still some ugly people around, aren't there?"

"You might be right," Ryan said.

"I have to be, least most of the time. Now—anything else on your mind?"

Ryan realized he was being dismissed. "No, I guess that's it." He got up and walked over to where his raincoat was draped over the back of a chair. "I'll follow up on the girl." What else would he be doing? He wanted to say something, calm and matter-of-fact, and that was all he could think of.

"I'm going to be out of town a few days," Mr. Perez said. "But Raymond'll be here. Not right *here,* but he'll let you know where he's staying. Let's get it done and we'll all go someplace where it's warm. How's that sound?"

It sounded to Ryan like the principal talking again, patting him on the head. He didn't like the feeling that came with the man's patronizing tone. The man probably didn't realize what he sounded like, thinking he was putting one over on the clucks—the dumb process server—with his easygoing one-of-the-boys delivery. Ryan had suspected it the first time they met, getting the feel of the man. Now he was sure of it. Hiding inside the gentleman from Baton Rouge was a pretty cold and heartless son of a bitch.

Ryan's second insertion in the personal columns of the *News* and *Free Press* appeared the day after Robert Leary was found shot to death and his wife disappeared. Ryan had almost called the papers to cancel the insertions if he could, then changed his mind. The notice said:

> BOBBY LEAR
> MONEY
> - waiting with your
> name on it. Contact
> Box 5388

Virgil Royal read the notice and said, Shit.

He should have waited to see what the man wanted with Bobby, though it had felt good, what he'd done...walking into the Montcalm Hotel whore joint with his raincoat on and knit cap down over his head. He didn't have to scare the night clerk any, because the night clerk didn't give a shit, he was mostly drunk

and looked like he had been mostly drunk and wearing
the same shirt and pants twenty years. He took the ten-
dollar bill, Virgil almost seeing him translating it into
two fifths and a six-pack, and said, "I believe the party
you're looking for's in 312. Light-skinned gentleman—"

"Where is that, in the front? Three-twelve?"

The night clerk had to stop and think. "It's on the
left, toward the back."

Bet to it—on the side with the fire escape, by the
parking lot. Virgil was counting on it for his cute idea
to work—room with a fire escape out the window. It
wouldn't be all luck. Virgil would bet the shotgun under
his raincoat Bobby's room had two ways to get out.

He took the elevator up to the fourth floor, walked
down the hall and knocked on 412.

A woman's voice, irritated, said, "What do you want?"

"Nothing," Virgil said.

He took the stairs up to the fifth floor and knocked
on 512. No answer. He knocked a couple more times
before taking out his ring of keys and finding one that
fit. Entering the room, he felt his patience paying off
again—thinking, doing it the easy way—seeing the
window in the darkness, the square of outside light and
the rungs of the fire escape. Virgil took off his shoes.
He went down the fire escape two floors with the shotgun in his hand, edged up to the window of 312, then
past the drawn shade to the railing, reached out, and
laid the sawed-off Hi-Standard twelve-gauge on the sill
of the frosted-glass bathroom window.

It seemed like it was taking a lot of time, but that's
the way it was, being patient. He could've poked the
shotgun through the glass and blown Bobby out of bed.
He'd decided, though, he'd rather talk to the man first,
ask him a question. Not while he was holding a shotgun
on him. No, the way to do it, while Bobby had a gun
and felt he was the boss.

Virgil remembered almost changing his mind, standing there at 312. Then he was knocking and it was too
late to back out. Close to the door, he said, "Hey, Bobby?
It's me, Virgil," keeping his voice low.

It didn't take too long after that.

Once Bobby Lear was sure it was only Virgil, nobody backing him up, he had to play his Bobby Lear part: take the chain off and let him in, holding a nickel-plated .38 he could trim his mustache in, not pointed right at Virgil, holding it loose once Virgil's raincoat was off and he'd given him a quick feel for metal objects.

Bobby asked him how he was doing. Virgil told him fine, there was nothing like going to bed at ten and eating home-cooked prison chow to make a person fit, was there? Bobby said that was the truth. Virgil asked him whatever happened to Wendell Haines and Bobby said Wendell had died. Virgil said he heard something like that, but who was it shot him? Bobby said it beat the shit out of him. Probably the police. Virgil said how come he was living in the Montcalm Hotel, on account of all the cute ladies? Bobby said that was it. Five floors of pussy. Virgil said, You hiding from somebody? Bobby said, It look like I am? Virgil said, Uh-huh. Bobby said, From who? Virgil said, From me. That got him to the question.

"Something I been waking up at night wondering," Virgil said. "How much we get from the Wyandotte Savings?"

Bobby seemed loose, leaning with his arm along the top of the dresser and the nickel plated .38 hanging limp in his hand. He had his pants on, his shirt hanging open, no shoes or socks. Very loose. But Virgil knew his eyes, the way he was staring. The man was here talking, but thinking about something else, making up his mind. Like a little kid's open expression.

"We didn't get nothing," Bobby said.

Virgil nodded, very slowly. "That's what I was afraid you were going to say. Nothing from the cashier windows?"

"Nothing," Bobby said. "No time."

"I heard seventeen big big ones."

"You heard shit."

"Told to me by honest gentlemen work for the prosecuting attorney."

"Told to you by your mama it still shit."

"Well, no use talking about it, is there?"

"Let me ask you something," Bobby said. "You put

that in the paper to me? Call this number?"

"No, I wondered you might think it was me," Virgil said. "It somebody else looking for you."

"How you know about it?"

"I saw it, same as you did. I saw the man that put it in."

"What's he want?"

"Man looking for you—I thought maybe you owed him money, too."

"You telling me I owe you money? On the Wyandotte?"

Got him up, now push him a little.

"You owe me *something*,"Virgil said. "Or I owe you something. One or the other."

"Shit," Bobby said. "I think somebody give me the wrong information. You the one, Virgil, should be staying here. You all fucked up in your head, acting strange."

"Wait right there," Virgil said.

Bobby straightened up. "Where you going?"

Virgil was moving toward the bathroom. "Make wee-wee. That all right?"

"Don't touch the coat."

"Hey, it's cool," Virgil said. "Take it easy." He went into the bathroom, turned on the light and swung the door almost closed. There was nothing more to talk about. Bobby knew it. Bobby would have a load in the chamber of the nickel plate and he might have already decided on his move. You couldn't tell about Bobby. He could try it right now or in a week, or wake up a month from now in the mood. That's why Virgil eased open the frosted-glass window and got the twelve-gauge from the sill.

Nothing cute now, the cute part was over. He'd like to take the time to see Bobby's face, but not with the man holding his shiny gun.

Virgil used his foot to bring the bathroom door in, out of the way. He stepped into the opening and gave Bobby a load dead-center that pinned him against the dresser and gave Virgil time to pump and bust him again, the sound coming out in a hard heavy *wham-wham* double-O explosion that Virgil figured, grinning about it later, must have rocked some whores out of bed. Virgil picked up the nickel-plated .38, wiped it clean on Bobby's pants, and took it with him.

But he should have waited. As good as it felt hitting Bobby, it didn't pay anything in prize money. He should have waited to see what this other money was about.

Bobby Lear. Money waiting with your name on it.

Then look at it another way. Dead or not, Bobby still owed him something. If he couldn't collect from Bobby, then how about from his wife?

Virgil sat down and closed his eyes to meditate, think it out.

Something was going on between the wife and the ofay man who'd been looking for Bobby. Name of Ryan. Virgil had the name and the man's phone number on a piece of paper in his wallet. He'd remember the name, anyway. Standing close to the drunk old man who'd called the number for him—sour-smelling old shitface bum who told him, drinking the two doubles, how he loved colored people, saying they were like little children to him—standing close, smelling the man, he'd heard Ryan say the name and repeat it and then spell it. Virgil knew he'd remember the name because it was the same as the name of a stripper he had seen at the Gaiety when he was a boy, Sunny Ryan, and she was the first white lady he had ever wanted to fuck. It was funny how you remembered things.

Now the wife and the man name of Ryan both knew from the paper Bobby was dead. But something else was still alive that had to do with money. That part was hard to understand. If the man knew Bobby was dead, how come he put the second one in the papers? *Money waiting.* Or maybe he didn't know Bobby was dead when he put it in. But wouldn't the money still be waiting? If the money was for Bobby, would his wife get it now? Maybe. If it was like money left to him.

The only thing to do, Virgil decided in his patience, was go see Bobby's wife. Buy her some wine and ask her what she knew about it. If she didn't know anything, then call up the man and sound real nice and arrange to meet him. Ask him the question. What's this money with Bobby's name on it? And if it sounded like the man was blowing smoke, pick him up and shake it out of him.

It turned out to be easier than Virgil Royal thought it would. He went out looking for Bobby's wife and at the first stop ran into the man name of Ryan.